Zachary held out his hand toward her son, ignoring her. "I'm Zachary."

Jordan's throat tightened. She swallowed several times, preparing herself for an onslaught of questions—possibly accusations—if her son gave his full name.

"I'm Nicholas." He fit his small hand in the large one.

"It's good to meet you, Nicholas. I think I've got the perfect little mare for you."

As her son followed Zachary toward the barn, relief fluttered down Jordan's length.

"So you and my mom know each other."

"Yeah, a long time ago." Zachary glanced back at her.

Why had she listened to her sister and come out here?

No matter how much she berated herself and the circumstances she found herself in, she would have to deal with Zachary—at least for the next hour. After that she could hightail it out of here—before he found out Nicholas was his son.

Books by Margaret Daley

Love Inspired	Love Inspired Suspense
*Gold in the Fire	So Dark the Night
*A Mother for Cindy	Vanished
*Light in the Storm	Buried Secrets
The Cinderella Plan	Don't Look Back
*When Dreams Come True	Forsaken Canyon
*Tidings of Joy	What Sarah Saw
**Once Upon a Family	Poisoned Secrets
**Heart of the Family	Cowboy Protector
**Family Ever After	
A Texas Thanksgiving	
**Second Chance Family	
**Together for the Holidays	
†Love Lessons	
†Heart of a Cowboy	

*The Ladies of Sweetwater Lake
**Fostered by Love
†Helping Hands Homeschooling

MARGARET DALEY

feels she has been blessed. She has been married more than thirty years to her husband, Mike, whom she met in college. He is a terrific support and her best friend. They have one son, Shaun. Margaret has been writing for many years and loves to tell a story. When she was a little girl, she would play with her dolls and make up stories about their lives. Now she writes these stories down. She especially enjoys weaving stories about families and how faith in God can sustain a person when things get tough. When she isn't writing, she is fortunate to be a teacher for students with special needs. Margaret has taught for more than twenty years and loves working with her students. She has also been a Special Olympics coach and has participated in many sports with her students.

Heart of a Cowboy
Margaret Daley

Steeple
Hill®

Published by Steeple Hill Books™

STEEPLE HILL BOOKS

Steeple
Hill®

Recycling programs
for this product may
not exist in your area.

ISBN-13: 978-0-373-87609-9

HEART OF A COWBOY

Copyright © 2010 by Margaret Daley

All rights reserved. Except for use in any review, the reproduction
or utilization of this work in whole or in part in any form by any
electronic, mechanical or other means, now known or hereafter
invented, including xerography, photocopying and recording, or in
any information storage or retrieval system, is forbidden without
the written permission of the editorial office, Steeple Hill Books,
233 Broadway, New York, NY 10279 U.S.A.

This is a work of fiction. Names, characters, places and incidents are
either the product of the author's imagination or are used fictitiously, and
any resemblance to actual persons, living or dead, business establishments,
events or locales is entirely coincidental.

This edition published by arrangement with Steeple Hill Books.

® and TM are trademarks of Steeple Hill Books, used under license.
Trademarks indicated with ® are registered in the United States Patent
and Trademark Office, the Canadian Trade Marks Office and in other
countries.

www.SteepleHill.com

Printed in U.S.A.

The Lord is good, a stronghold in the day of trouble; and He knoweth them that trust in Him.

—*Nahum* 1:7

To Ashley, Alexa, Abbey and Aubrey

Chapter One

The horse in the corral reared up, jerking the rope from his wrangler's grip. Standing next to the hood of her car watching the interplay, Jordan Masterson stiffened. The animal's hooves plunged down toward the man. Barely missing him.

She gasped. Even from a distance the flare of the animal's nostrils indicated agitation. She glanced at her ten-year-old son as he climbed from her yellow Camaro.

Nicholas can't ride. He could get hurt.

The horse's whinny drew her attention to the corral again. The huge black animal backed up, lifting its head as it stared wide-eyed at the cowboy.

"Whoa, boy. Easy, Midnight." The soothing cadence of the man's deep, husky voice eased the mounting tension in Jordan as well as the horse.

The animal slowed its backward steps. Its dilated pupils contracted. The man moved in closer, all the while saying, "Easy, boy. You're okay," until the horse stopped. The man raised his hand inch by slow inch. Finally his fingers grazed the horse's neck. He reached out and grasped the rope.

Something stirred deep in her memory. The cowboy's

back was to her, but Jordan noted the breadth of his shoulders, the narrow hips, the long legs, clad in dusty jeans and his worn brown boots. She ran her gaze up his well-built body to his nape where his sable hair curled against the collar of his white shirt.

"Mom, did you see that?"

"Yeah," she whispered, more to herself than anyone.

The cowboy turned partially toward them, and Jordan drew in a deep breath and held it. His square jaw, his alert stance prodded a memory forward—one she wanted to forget. She zeroed in on his face, but his black cowboy hat shadowed most of his features until he lifted his head enough for her to see the firm set of his full lips, the tic in his jawline, the frown that graced his expression. Panic seized her, tightening its squeeze on her lungs. A panic that had nothing to do with the temperamental horse in the corral.

Zachary Rutgers.

Her high school sweetheart. The man who broke her heart.

His sea-green gaze zoomed in on hers. Suddenly Jordan was whisked back eleven years to the last time she saw that scowl that now transformed his tanned features into a hardened countenance. Even from yards away the tension that poured off him blasted her.

Breath trapped, Jordan pivoted away, gripping the frame of the car door. "Nicholas, maybe you shouldn't learn to ride right now." She schooled her voice into a level tone while inside her heartbeat galloped like a runaway stallion.

"Ah, Mom, you promised I could when we moved here."

"But…" *I can't do this. We can't be around Zachary.*

"I really want to ride."

Her son's intense stare drilled into her, reminding her

yet again of the promise she'd made. One she needed to break.

"You said I should do something physical."

Her own reasoning was going to come back and bite her. Nicholas was a child who would stay buried in his books if she didn't get him out of the house and doing some activities. He was ten but was more comfortable around adults. His genius-level IQ often made him the butt of other kids' jokes. Something she had hoped would change when they'd moved back to Tallgrass. It hadn't.

"Hon, let me ask around. I'm sure there are other places you can get some riding lessons." Just not at this ranch. Not with this cowboy.

Her son swiveled toward the corral and grinned at Zachary, who was striding toward them.

"Jordan, I didn't realize you were back in town."

I didn't realize you were, either. "Yeah, I moved back a few weeks ago. When did you and your wife move back?"

"Wife? I'm not married."

He looked from her to her son. "What can I do for you?"

Not married? But he had been engaged.

"Aunt Rachel said you give riding lessons out here." Nicholas straightened his shoulders. "I want to learn to ride. Maybe be in a rodeo one day."

Rodeo? Where had that come from? Jordan's panic, centered on Zachary, suddenly shifted to her son. Participating in rodeos was dangerous.

Zachary pushed his hat back from his forehead. "Well, partner, the only lessons I give are for the kids in the Helping Hands Homeschooling group. Are you part of that?"

Nicholas threw a glance back at her. "Mom?"

A homeschooling group? Jordan heaved a sigh and

slammed the car door, then rounded the front of her Camaro. "No, we aren't. Sorry to bother you." She had intended to grasp her son's hand and get out of there as quickly as possible. Before any questions were asked. Why hadn't her sister and mother told her Zachary was living in Tallgrass?

Nicholas stepped out of her reach and even closer to the fence that separated him from Zachary. "May I see some of the horses? I've never been on a ranch." His grin grew to encompass his whole face. "I've read all about how a ranch works and how to train horses."

Zachary slid a glance toward her, his gaze boring into her for a full minute. Behind the hard glint a hundred questions lurked—ones she didn't want to answer. Her own anger bubbled to the surface and shoved the panic down. He was the one who had gotten engaged so soon after their breakup.

"Please, mister."

Zachary wrenched his attention from Jordan. His face relaxed its harshness, and he actually smiled clear to the green depths of those eyes that had captured her interest when she'd been a junior in high school.

"Tell you what. I have three kids coming out to ride. They should be here soon. If it's okay with your mother, you can join them this time."

No, it isn't okay. The words screamed through Jordan's mind while her son swung around with that puppy-dog look that turned her to mush.

"Mom, may I please?"

Only her son would ask and be grammatically correct. Zachary's gaze fell on her, too, and she resisted the urge to squirm. In the end he was the one who had walked away from their relationship. And she wasn't going to let him make her feel guilty.

Jordan tilted up her chin and looked Zachary square in the face. "That would be fine. I appreciate your making an exception this once. Shouldn't you run it by your boss first, though?"

He lowered his hat to shield his eyes. "I own the Wild Bill Buffalo Ranch."

His answer really didn't surprise her since Zachary used to spend time at his uncle's ranch in southern Oklahoma. Had he fulfilled his dream of being a bull rider on the rodeo circuit? What happened to the woman his mother said he was engaged to? There was so much she didn't know about him now—purposefully.

"C'mon. I'll get you hitched up with a horse and give you a few pointers before the others arrive." Zachary moved a few steps to the gate of the corral and opened it. "I'm Zachary." He held out his hand toward her son, ignoring her.

Jordan's throat tightened. She swallowed several times, preparing herself for an onslaught of questions—possibly accusations—if her son gave his full name.

"I'm Nicholas." He fit his small hand in the large one.

"It's good to meet you, Nicholas. Let's go. I think I've got the perfect little mare for you."

As her son followed Zachary toward the barn, relief fluttered down her length. Nicholas's undersize frame fooled many people into thinking he was younger than ten. In this case, she was glad because it gave her time to decide what to do about the fact that she and Zachary now lived in the same town again.

"So you and my mom know each other."

"Yeah, a long time ago. We went to school together." Zachary glanced back at her.

His limp as he entered the barn caught her attention. A riding accident? The second the question popped into her mind, she shook it away. She didn't want to know the answer to that query. She didn't want to have anything to do with him.

At the entrance Nicholas stopped and waited for her to catch up. Reluctantly she hurried toward him. Why out of all the activities and sports she had mentioned to him did Nicholas pick riding horses? Why had she listened to her sister and come out here? She suspected she knew what Rachel was up to and would have a word about her meddling.

No matter how much she berated herself and the circumstances she found herself in, she would have to deal with Zachary—at least for the next hour. After that she could hightail it out of here—before he found out Nicholas was his son.

Ever since Zachary had come back to Tallgrass, his past with Jordan would sneak into his thoughts, his dreams. He'd found himself wondering about her more and more. Now she was here at his ranch. He hadn't been prepared for her surprise visit. Memories—both good and bad— overwhelmed him as he glanced back at Jordan with her son. Her life had gone on just fine without him.

Her son was what? Around eight? Obviously Jordan hadn't wasted any time finding a replacement for him. His gut solidified like the hard ground when he was thrown from a horse. His leg aching more than usual, Zachary stalked toward the stall to fetch a horse for the boy to ride.

Zachary led the mare into the center of the barn. He certainly had a right to be mad at her. She'd left him. Not the other way around. When she'd received the scholarship to the art school in Savannah, he'd tried to be happy for her. But there was a good one within a few hours of Tallgrass, and yet she'd decided to go to the college in Georgia. He'd given her his heart, and she'd left it to spend four years at a place halfway across the country.

The night before she'd left for Savannah, they had a huge fight. Their views of their future together had been so different, and she'd decided to break it off with him. They needed their space. He'd waited two months for her to change her mind. Then when he couldn't stay in Tallgrass another moment, he'd joined the army. He'd needed to get away to decide what he wanted to do with the rest of his life.

And he'd never heard from her after that—until now. Eleven long years later. Too late for them.

Chapter Two

"Mom, are you okay?" Nicholas asked as he stood in the barn entrance.

Jordan cut the distance between them, the odors of dust and musky grass squeezing her throat. "Seeing that horse in the corral reminded me how dangerous riding can be." But even worse was seeing Zachary again. Now she was faced with several dilemmas. The first being should she tell Zachary he was Nicholas's father and change everything? It had been so long. She didn't know if she could.

"I'll be all right. I'm tougher than I look." Her son puffed out his chest.

"I know, honey, but this really isn't a good idea. Let's thank him and leave."

"Mom, you're babying me again. I'm ten years old."

Jordan's gaze zoomed in on Zachary leading a horse out of a stall, hoping he hadn't heard how old Nicholas was. She couldn't have the conversation she knew she now had to have in the middle of a barn with her son looking on. This wasn't the time or the place—if ever there was one. But she would have to soon on her terms. After all, Zachary walked away from her, refusing to return her calls.

"Fine. But if I think it's getting too dangerous, you'll get off immediately and that will be the end of riding." A few years ago, she'd almost lost Nicholas. She wouldn't lose him now.

"I know what you're thinking. My atrial septal defect has been fixed. My cardiologist says I'm fit as a fiddle. While I never thought of a fiddle as especially being fit, the point he's making is I'm fine now."

Jordan shook her head. There wasn't much she could get past her child. She flitted her hands. "Go. Have fun." For now. She'd find something else he'd enjoy that would give him some physical activity to make him forget about the horses.

"I will." Nicholas covered the short distance to Zachary, who had the chestnut mare already saddled and ready to go.

"There's a mounting block outside that you can use." Zachary led the horse out the back double doors, never once looking her way since he'd left her standing by the corral.

Jordan trailed after the pair, wanting to be close for Nicholas but far away because of Zachary and his possible questions. *Lord, what do I tell him? He wanted nothing to do with me after we broke up that summer after graduation.*

Before she knew it, her son was sitting on a horse that was huge. If he fell off, the ground would be a long way down and the impact would be hard. As Zachary gave Nicholas a few instructions on how to sit properly in the saddle, use the reins and get the animal to do what her son wanted, Jordan stepped a little closer to the paddock where they were. Zachary walked beside Nicholas and the mare as they circled the corral.

The deep timbre in Zachary's voice as he explained to

her son what to do flowed over her, prodding memories forward of those fun times they had shared before everything had fallen apart. The memory of the feel of his long fingers as they combed through her hair or the brush of his lips over hers sent her heart beating faster.

She jerked back from the fence, putting some space between them. She would not fall for Zachary Rutgers again. Even if he was Nicholas's father and not married now, she would keep her distance. If she never told him about Nicholas being his son, then it would be easy to keep away. If she did, they would be connected always.

Zachary glanced toward the entrance into the barn. "Ah, I see the others are here." As he peered away, his look brushed over her, reminding her again of the soft feel of his lips grazing hers. "Sit here for a few minutes, partner. I'll be right back."

After tying the horse to the fence, he passed her striding toward the large double doors. His gaze homed in on her, his eyes narrow, his mouth set in a tight line. The we'll-talk-later stare held her rooted to the ground although her first inclination was to whirl around and flee. Again her anger flooded her. He acted as if he hadn't done anything wrong. She refused to break the visual connection first.

He looked toward the barn when a child called out his name. His steps lengthened, and he quickly disappeared inside. Jordan let out a long breath and sank against the fence post nearby, her legs weak, her hands shaking.

"Isn't this cool, Mom?"

Her son's question forced her to pull herself together. She was discovering how much anger she still had toward Zachary for leaving her when she'd needed him the most.

"You might hold the saddle horn." She moved toward the mare. If he fell, maybe she could catch him before he hit the ground. She'd remembered Zachary once having a broken arm from being thrown from a horse, and then there had been the accident at the Oklahoma Junior Rodeo Finals. Him lying crumpled in the dirt. The dust created from the horse finally settling around Zachary's prone body. Whatever had possessed her to agree to come out here in the first place? She hadn't really thought the riding lessons out.

Zachary approached with three kids. "Nicholas, this is Jana, Randy and Ashley. They'll be riding with us."

Her son greeted each one as they led their horses out of the barn to mount. His grin spoke of his joy and pushed Jordan's fears to the background. She'd be right here as he rode around in the paddock. She'd be right here to make sure he didn't go faster than a walk.

"Uncle Zachary, can we go for a ride to the stream?" Ashley sat atop her mare, her dark brown hair pulled back in a ponytail.

Randy swung up into the saddle. "Yeah, it's getting hot today. It'd be fun wading in the water. Can we?"

"I don't know. Nicholas is just learning." Zachary rubbed his hand along the stubble of growth on his jaw.

"But I did my first time riding." Jana took off her cowboy hat and fanned her face.

"I'd love to go for a ride. Please." Her son threw in his own plea.

"Let me get my horse." Zachary started for the barn.

Jordan stepped into his path. "Nicholas doesn't know how to ride. He can't go." Over his shoulder, she could see the hopeful look on her son's face fall.

The intensity in Zachary's eyes bored through her as though it could make her move away. "He'll be okay. But he's your son."

Yes, he was. She'd been in labor for thirty-six hours alone. She'd raised him alone. Watched him go through the surgery to repair his heart defect alone. "He'd never been on a horse until fifteen minutes ago." She hated the fact she felt as though she had to justify her stance.

"If I remember correctly when I taught you how to ride, we went riding in a meadow not long after that. Doing it in a paddock isn't what I really call riding."

She remembered one time when they had ridden across a pasture, galloping, the wind blowing through her long, loose hair. And they had ended up kissing for the first time under a large oak tree when they had finally stopped. Heat flushed her cheeks at the remembrance of his lips on hers.

"He'll be okay, Jordan. Nothing ever happened to you riding."

"But it did to you."

"If it'll make you feel better, come with us." His voice held no emotion. It was as though she were a stranger to him.

"I haven't ridden in years."

"It'll come back to you." He skirted around her and strode into the barn.

Chewing her bottom lip, Jordan peered at her son, who patted his mare. Should she go?

When Nicholas stared behind her, his face brightened. Jordan swept around and saw Zachary leading two horses out of the barn. He handed the reins of one to her, their hands brushing against each other. His eyes widened for a few seconds as he peered down at where they had briefly connected. With a shake of his head, he quickly stepped away and swung up into the saddle of his mount.

He'd felt the electric jolt just as she had. She massaged her fingertips into her palm, trying to erase his touch. It had been nearly impossible as a teenager and still was.

She glanced at her son then at the mare next to her. "Okay, I'll come along."

"Yippee!" Nicholas shouted, pumping one arm into the air.

Ashley rode in the lead with Jana next to her. Randy followed with Nicholas slightly behind him and to the side. Zachary waited for Jordan to go next then took up the rear. As they crossed the meadow, heading toward a grove of trees, the feel of Zachary's gaze zapped a fiery trail down her spine. In less than an hour in his presence, he tempted her to forget eleven years of heartache. No, she wouldn't let him get close this time.

She listened to her son talk with the other children, who willingly answered his questions about Key Elementary although all of them were homeschooled. Nicholas had only been attending the school for ten days. He hadn't said much to her, but she sensed the same teasing was happening there that had at his previous one in South Carolina. Her son was a scholar and a pacifist besides being a grade ahead and small. She'd questioned him on the way out to the ranch about how school was going, and he had gone silent. A sure sign something was wrong with her talkative son.

"He'll be all right." Zachary came alongside her.

She slowed the horse's gait and let the kids get a little farther ahead because she didn't want Nicholas to overhear anything that might lead to questions—at least not until she knew what she was going to do about Zachary. She'd tried to tell him about Nicholas, but when he hadn't returned her calls, she'd decided she could do it without him. She would never force anyone into a relationship he didn't want. "Who?" she finally asked although she knew he was referring to her son.

"Nicholas."

She wasn't so sure Nicholas would be all right. A couple of kids at his last school had been awful to him, making his life so miserable that she decided to move back home before school started in August. She was tired of doing everything without any family support, and her mother had said she needed help with Granny. Now at least she had her mother, grandmother and sister here. In all those eleven years, she'd only returned to Tallgrass a couple of times, the last time two years ago when her sister's husband died unexpectedly from a heart attack.

"He's a natural when it comes to riding. He knows instinctively how to flow with his horse."

Jordan studied Nicholas for a moment and had to agree. He was a natural—like his father.

"Are you always this uptight or is it just around me that you get that way?"

"Uptight?"

He gestured toward her hands gripping the reins. "Relax. Maybelle is sensitive to her rider."

"Do you blame me? We didn't exactly end our relationship on a good note."

He nodded his head toward Nicholas. "It looks like you found someone to replace me pretty fast. What's your son? Eight?" A tic twitched in his jawline, its strong set strengthening even more.

"How about you? I thought you would be married by now." The last time she'd called Zachary's mother to get hold of him, she would never forget the news the woman imparted before she could tell Zachary's mom about the baby. He was engaged to someone he served with in the army, and he was still stationed overseas. His mother might as well have said, "Out of your reach."

"No. Where's your husband?" His gaze held hers captive, a hard glitter to his eyes.

What happened to your fiancée? She bit the inside of her mouth to keep the words inside. She wouldn't let him know how much that had hurt her when she'd discovered he'd moved on only seven months after they had broken up. "I'm not married."

"What happened to Nicholas's father?"

"He hasn't been in the picture for quite some time."

"Sorry to hear that—" he paused for a long moment "—for your son's sake."

But not mine. His unspoken words cut her to the core. The pain sliced through her in spite of her efforts to distance herself. Anger rose. "How long have you been back in Tallgrass?"

"A couple of years. Becca found this ranch for sale for me. The deal was too good to turn down."

"How's your sister?" Becca had been the first one she'd talked to when she'd called after the doctor had told her she was pregnant. She'd only been at art school in Savannah for two and a half months. The news had rocked her world, and she hadn't known what to do. She'd desperately needed to talk with Zachary, but he'd enlisted in the army and was at boot camp. Becca had promised her she would tell Zachary to call. He never did.

"She's still married to the same man, and they have three kids. They live here on the ranch, too. Ashley is the oldest."

Jordan glanced toward the children. Zachary's niece slid from her horse and tied its rein on a tree limb. Jordan nudged her mare to go faster as Jana and Randy dismounted, too. Her son started to bring his leg over and drop to the ground.

"Hold it, Nicholas," she shouted, mentally measuring the long distance from the horse to the patch of grass below the mare. "I'll help you."

"Jordan, he's doing fine. Let him do it himself. That's the way he'll learn."

She slanted a look toward Zachary. "But…"

"See." Zachary pointed toward her son, who'd slipped to the ground and like the others was tying up his horse. "Why are you so protective?"

"That's how mothers are supposed to be." She'd come so close to losing Nicholas. She didn't know what she would have done if he'd died. He was her world.

"Yes, protect but not smother."

"What do you know about being a parent?" Her hands curled around the reins, and she pulled harder than she should have to halt the mare. He hadn't wanted children, or at least that was the impression she'd gotten when they had talked about the future right after high school graduation. At the time, his dreams had centered around the rodeo—not having a family.

A flicker of pain glinted in his eyes before a frown descended. "You're right. I don't have personal experience raising a child, but I was a boy once. I know he needs a little breathing room."

He dismounted and strode away from her before she could think of a retort, some kind of defense for herself. She shouldn't have lashed out at him. He was right. Nicholas had told her that on more than one occasion, especially when she'd wanted to march up to the last school and face those kids who'd teased Nicholas and made fun of him. If it had started again, she would have to do something different. She wouldn't let her son be miserable for another school year.

Zachary stood at the edge of the stream that ran through his property and watched the kids wade across it. Their giggles peppered the air and brought a smile to his mouth.

He'd enjoyed living near his niece and nephews, but at night he always went home to an empty house with no child's laughter to fill it or bedtime stories to tell. And yet, Jordan had moved on with her life and had all of that with Nicholas.

The boy captured his attention as he bent down and stared at something on the ground. He picked it up and straightened. When he saw Zachary staring at him, Jordan's son crossed the creek and approached him.

"Look what I found. This is a *Terrapene carolina triunguis.*" Nicholas held it up for Zachary to see. His expression must have conveyed surprise because the child added, "A three-toed box turtle. They were common where I used to live. They eat insects, worms, fish, berries, snakes."

"Did you have one as a pet?"

"No. They're better off in their natural habitat. I have a dog named Tucker."

What eight-year-old kid knew the scientific name of a turtle? At least he assumed that was what the child spouted off. "Do you like science a lot?"

Nicholas shrugged. "It's okay. I really enjoy math the most. I've been working on algebra, but tell you a secret—" he leaned toward Zachary "—Mom's not very good at it. I have to teach myself."

"Teach yourself? That's mighty ambitious."

"I love to learn." Nicholas set the turtle on the ground. *Like his mother.* Jordan had always been a good student while he'd been more interested in sports, especially riding. She'd helped him with his classwork and he'd taught her to ride. For a brief moment he allowed himself to recall some of the good times he and Jordan had in high school— when she'd helped him cram for a test and he'd made an A or when he'd worked odd jobs to save enough to buy her a necklace the first Christmas they'd been together.

The glimpse of her smile had made it all worth it. Randy's voice calling Nicholas pulled Zachary away from the past—thankfully. He didn't need to remember.

Jordan's son flashed him a smile. "Gotta go." He whirled and raced toward the other kids.

Zachary watched the children talking. Nicholas pointed at something in the creek and Jana squealed, ducking behind Randy. A brown, foot-long snake slithered through the water. Zachary slid his attention to Jordan. Her eyes grew round, and she backed away from the stream. She never did like snakes.

He chuckled, remembering that time he'd found one on her porch. She'd jumped into his arms so fast he'd staggered back, almost losing his balance. But he'd recovered and tightened his embrace, cradling her against him. The onslaught of memories cracked a fissure in the wall about his emotions.

Those carefree days were over. She'd walked away from him and never looked back.

"We better get back to the barn." Zachary started for his horse.

"Do we hafta, Uncle Zachary?"

He glanced at his niece. "Yeah, Alexa will be here to pick up Jana."

Nicholas had already crossed the stream while the other three were still on the opposite side. They reluctantly followed. For a few seconds a yearning for what he didn't have inundated Zachary. But he pushed it aside. He just had to be satisfied with having a niece and two nephews. And staying out of Jordan's way.

Chapter Three

Sore, Jordan slid to the ground back at the barn half an hour later, keeping her eye on her son to make sure he dismounted okay. He did, almost like a pro. She had to admit everything Nicholas did he did well. He was quick to pick up things. But usually they weren't physical activities.

Jordan caught sight of Zachary taking a few extra moments to explain to her son how to take care of his horse after a ride. Nicholas absorbed what Zachary told him with his usual intense concentration. She knew that after this he wouldn't have to be told again. Zachary patted him on the shoulder. The smile her son gave Zachary right before he strode away to tend to his gelding stirred doubts in her that she hadn't made a good choice all those years ago.

That brief scene confirmed she had to tell Zachary about Nicholas soon. There was no way she could keep her secret if they were both living in such a small town. He was bound to find out some way or another. She still didn't know how she would break the news. Tell Zachary first or Nicholas? She felt in over her head. But maybe this was one of the reasons she'd finally come home. She wanted Nicholas to be surrounded by family—even Zachary's. It would be to her son's benefit, and maybe for once, she wouldn't feel so alone in this world. Yes, she'd always had the support of her mother, grandmother and sister, but long-distance support wasn't the same as immediate face-to-face interactions. And yet, for years she'd lived far away from that support because of her feelings toward Zachary.

Could she really tell him? If she kept quiet, she wouldn't have to see him. She could even leave Tallgrass. He never had to know. That idea suddenly appealed to her because every time she thought of telling him about Nicholas, her stomach coiled into a hard ball.

"Hi. Jana told me your son had his first riding lesson today." A young woman with long, curly mahogany hair and soft, dark brown eyes stopped next to Jordan. "I'm Alexa Ferguson, Jana's stepmom."

Jordan shook the hand the twentysomething offered her. "Nice to meet you. My son enjoyed getting to know Jana and the others. He can be shy around new kids."

"So can Jana, but this year she's come a long way."

"How so?"

"The best thing my husband did for Jana was take her out of school and teach her at home. She'd developed separation anxiety when her mother divorced Ian and left. She was afraid she was going to lose him, too. She needed that time with her father. I don't advocate that for every child because a school placement is right for a lot of them, but some need something else. Jana was one of those."

"So you think homeschooling is a good option for some?" *Is that what Nicholas needs?*

"Jana has blossomed since she's been at home. When I'm not taking classes, I help Ian teach her. This past couple of weeks, I haven't had a chance as much since I'm doing my student teaching, and to tell you the truth, I miss working with her."

"So it's been a positive experience?"

"It's been great. I'm finishing my elementary education degree, so it's a good experience for me. She's bright, and we've had so much fun." Alexa hiked her large purse up on her shoulder.

"But you know what you're doing." She didn't know the first thing about homeschooling. What if homeschooling was the answer if Nicholas continued to have problems at school? She'd never studied to be a teacher like Alexa. How could she teach her child with his high IQ? But she should check into it.

"The beauty of being part of the Helping Hands Homeschooling group is you have support from other parents who are doing the same thing and have probably gone through the same problems. Most of them don't have formal educational training."

"Zachary mentioned something about being involved with the organization."

"Are you thinking of homeschooling your son?"

Jordan searched the area and found Nicholas talking with Randy, both boys relaxed, grinning. "I never thought about that option for him until now." She didn't know what to do. Going up to the school, talking with the teacher and principal really hadn't taken care of what Nicholas had needed at his last school.

"Why don't you come to an HHH meeting this week and talk with others who've been involved a long time. I've only been doing it since January."

Jana ran up to Alexa. "Can Ashley come home with us today?"

"Sure. Your dad is working on the bench for your room so he'll be busy in the garage." After Jana whirled around and raced to her friend, Alexa returned her attention to Jordan. "I hope I'll see you Wednesday night. I'll introduce you to some of the others." She rummaged in her big purse, pulled out a pad of paper and wrote an address down on it. "This is where we have our meetings."

Jordan stuffed the note into her jeans pocket. She just might take Alexa up on her offer, especially if her son continued to have social problems. Yesterday morning, his second Friday, he hadn't wanted to go because of a stomachache, but today he'd had a great time interacting with the kids at the ranch.

After Alexa gathered Jana and Ashley to leave, Jordan called out for Nicholas to get into the car. Then she crossed to where Zachary stood by the corral with the horse that had been frightened earlier. He glanced at her when she came up to the railing next to him.

At the stream after he'd stomped off, they hadn't said a word to each other, but she needed to thank him at least. Soon enough their rocky relationship could be even rockier if she told him about Nicholas. "Thanks for letting us stay and for giving Nicholas a riding lesson."

"No problem." He kept his arms resting on a slat of the fence, his gaze trained on the horse in the paddock. "Even though I don't have any children, I love having them here at the ranch."

Ouch! The jab at her earlier statement scored a direct hit, especially when he did have a child although he didn't know it. "I'm sorry I said that. It's obvious children respond to you. The kids enjoyed the ride today, especially Nicholas."

"And that's why he's welcome to come out here and ride. He doesn't have to be part of the homeschooling group for him to be included. I saw how much he enjoyed it." His tightly clasped hands attested to how much that invitation had cost him.

"Can I get back to you on that?"

"Sure. I'm here most days." He shoved himself away from the railing and turned toward her. "For the lessons you can just leave Nicholas and come back in an hour. Most parents don't stay."

There had been a time they had spent every possible moment together. Now it was obvious he didn't want to have anything to do with her. Which was the way she wanted it. What would he do when or if he discovered Nicholas was his son? For a few seconds she considered telling him and just getting it over with. The words were on the tip of her tongue. But she peered to her left and saw her son making a beeline for them. She didn't want everything to change with that revelation. She needed to do some thinking, praying.

"Thanks for the riding lesson. I haven't had that much fun in a long time."

If she had been thinking of refusing Zachary's invitation, her son's declaration stopped that.

"You're welcome to come anytime."

"Really? Great!" Nicholas beamed. "Mom, can I come next Saturday? The others will."

"We'll see. Right now we need to get home. Nana's gonna wonder where we disappeared to." Jordan started for her car.

"But Aunt Rachel knows. She'll tell her." Nicholas halted his progress toward the Camaro, swung toward Zachary and waved. "Bye. See you Saturday."

Jordan wanted to tell Nicholas no, but she knew she couldn't deny him an opportunity to ride, especially since it was his father who would be teaching him. As she pulled away from the barn, she glimpsed Zachary leaning back against the railing, studying her with those intense green eyes.

His last expression, totally unreadable, stayed with Jordan the whole way home. Twenty minutes later she pulled into the driveway of the two-story house where she'd grown up. Her sister lived down the street. After years away, she and Nicholas were finally surrounded by family members—more than she'd counted on when she'd decided to return to Tallgrass.

"I need to take care of Tucker. I'll be out back." Nicholas hopped from the car and raced toward the backyard and the dog that had been his companion through his ordeal to fix the hole in his heart.

Inside she found her mother lying down on the couch in the den with a cold pack on her forehead. Jordan started to back out of the room when her mom shot up.

"How did it go riding?"

Jordan sank into a chair, her muscles protesting the afternoon ride, her head pounding with tension from dealing with Zachary. "Why didn't you or Rachel tell me Zachary owned the ranch?"

Her mother's eyes widened. "Maybe your sister knew, but I didn't. I'd heard he was back in town, but that's all."

"Well, then, why didn't you tell me that at least?"

She swung her feet to the floor and faced Jordan. "Because I was afraid you wouldn't come home. Isn't he the reason you've stayed away?"

"My work kept me in South Carolina."

"Your graphics design business can be done from anywhere. You had a few clients there, but you've managed to serve them from here, haven't you?"

"Okay, you're right. Most of my clients are from all over."

"See, I knew it."

Jordan removed the rubber band that held her hair off her neck. She shook her curls loose, running her fingers through them. "It's hot out there."

"It's August in Oklahoma. That means hot. And you're avoiding talking about your encounter with Zachary."

"I didn't know that was what we were talking about. Why the cold pack?"

"Your grandmother is driving me crazy." Her mother frowned. "And you're doing it again. It's obvious you ran into Zachary. How did it go?"

"I've been manipulated by my son into taking him back out to the ranch for more lessons with Zachary as the instructor. Not something I'm looking forward to."

"Are you going to tell him about Nicholas?"

The question shot Jordan to her feet. She hurried to the entrance and checked to make sure her son wasn't anywhere he could overhear, then moved back to the chair and plopped down. "I don't want Nicholas to know until I'm ready to tell him. He thinks his father didn't want to be involved with us." Which was what she had convinced herself of. Now she wasn't so sure of anything. Even if Zachary found out about Nicholas, he might not want to be in his son's life, but after today she realized she probably should have pursued getting in touch with him more than a couple of times. But her feelings had been so hurt she couldn't bring herself to make another call that might go unreturned.

"He never questioned you about his father?" Her mother schooled her voice into a whisper.

"Sure, when he was young. I think he saw how upset I got by the subject that he decided not to ask any more questions."

"So what are you going to do?"

"That's a good question. One I need an answer to."

"Hon, you've got to figure that out yourself. I know it's been rough raising Nicholas by yourself, especially with his heart problem, but the doctor said he was fine now, that the surgery was a success. You've done a wonderful job with him."

"But, Mom, I've made some big mistakes." She was blessed to have Nicholas in her life and wouldn't trade him for anything. But a mistake she had been paying for these past eleven years was believing that she and Zachary would be together forever and giving herself to him before they were married.

"We all make mistakes. Remember Christ was the only person who walked this earth who was perfect. I'm not perfect. You aren't. Zachary isn't."

"I know, but in South Carolina I could forget that Zachary was the other half of Nicholas. Here I can't. I discovered that today. My past has caught up with me."

"Then you need to tell Zachary right away."

"I've got to find the right place and time. I want to tell Zachary before I say anything to Nicholas. I owe Zachary at least that much. I'm giving myself some time to figure it out. What to say. Where to say it. I'm not rushing into it. I've got to do it right."

Her mother pushed to her feet, clutching the cold pack. "You always have to analyze everything. You never rush into anything. Don't wait too long, hon. The truth needs to come from you and frankly Nicholas looks a lot like Zachary."

Her son's features were similar to Zachary's, but Nicholas's hair was blond and his stature was small like hers.

"As sharp as your son is, he might figure it out if given the time and given the connection between you two."

Jordan stood. "Okay, you've made your point." She couldn't have that. She needed to decide how and when.

"Now if I could only make my point with your grandma."

"What's going on with Granny?"

"She has a date tonight."

"What's wrong with that?"

"Don't you think eighty is a little old to start dating after being a widow for twenty-five years?"

Jordan chuckled. "It's wonderful. Where did she meet him?"

"At church. He's a widower. Doug Bateman lives down the street. She can barely walk without her walker, but I think she's been sneaking out to meet him in the park."

"She's an adult. I think she can do what she wants."

Her mother snorted, rounded the coffee table and crossed the den to the doorway. "I'm gonna see if I can get more support from your sister," she mumbled as she left the room.

Jordan eased into the chair again. The throbbing beat of her headache pulsated behind her eyes. She buried her face in her hands and massaged her fingertips into her forehead.

I need help, Lord. I don't know how to tell Zachary or Nicholas. Everything will change if I do.

"Ashley told me a new kid named Nicholas joined them today riding and his mother is Jordan. Do you have something to tell me?" Becca approached Zachary not an hour after Jordan had left the ranch with her son.

Zachary slanted a look at his sister standing on the other side of the corral fence with her hand on her hip. "Nope."

"The other day I heard *Jordan* Masterson came back to town. Was that her?"

"Why didn't you tell me she was back?" He removed his hat and tapped it against his jeans. "I don't like surprises."

"I didn't think she would come out here."

"So it was okay not to say anything to me? I was bound to meet her sometime in Tallgrass. We have a number of the same friends, and I'm sure she'll get reacquainted with them."

His older sister studied him. "I thought you had moved on."

He'd thought so, too. Until he'd seen Jordan and all the old hurt came back. His gut burned as if acid eroded it. "As much as I'm enjoying this little chitchat, I've got to train this horse." He gestured toward Midnight, warily watching him on the other side of the paddock.

Becca huffed, her mouth pinched into a frown. "If you need to talk, you know where the house is."

As his sister left, Zachary made his way toward Midnight. He'd wanted a family, children, and couldn't have any now. But in spite of the rodeo accident that snatched away his dream he'd carved out a life here in Tallgrass, and Jordan had come back and disrupted everything.

Why couldn't she just stay away? Leave him in peace? All those years ago he'd fled his hometown because every place he'd gone reminded him of Jordan. Even when he had joined the army—anything different to take his thoughts off Jordan—in the back of his mind he'd clung to the hope she would call and come back to him. She never did, and he was left to pick up the pieces. When he had patched his life back together, he'd vowed she would never break his heart again.

And now he'd gone and agreed to teach her son to ride. Now he would have to see Jordan once a week. He didn't want a weekly reminder of what could have been.

"Ms. Masterson, Nicholas seems to be having a hard time adjusting to this school. He knows the rules, and yet he snuck into the school at lunchtime when he was supposed to be outside on the playground. His teacher found him sitting at his desk when she came in after eating lunch."

Seated in front of the elementary school principal on Wednesday, Jordan crossed her legs, shifting to try to make herself more comfortable. But there was no way around it. She felt as though she'd been sent to the principal's office, rather than her son. "Was he disruptive or doing something he shouldn't in the room?"

"No, but that's not the point. He wasn't supposed to be there."

"Did you ask him why he came inside early?"

"He wouldn't say why." The principal scanned a piece of paper. "And I've got a report from the nurse that he's going to her almost every day complaining of a stomachache or something else being wrong. Have you taken him to the doctor to make sure he's all right?"

"Last week and he's fine." Jordan rose, gripping her purse in front of her like a firewall. "I'll talk with him." It was the same situation as his last school. He didn't fit in easily. She needed to do something to make his learning years more enjoyable.

As the older woman came to her feet, she leaned into her desk. "Maybe he shouldn't have skipped a grade."

"That's something the school in South Carolina did to keep him interested in his studies. The curriculum was too easy for him. Is he having problems academically?"

"On the contrary, his grades so far are excellent, but socially…" The principal averted her gaze for a moment then reestablished eye contact and said, "Frankly, he doesn't interact with the other children much. I'm concerned about him."

"Thank you. I'll talk with Nicholas today about following the rules." Her son always followed the rules. Which made this new behavior troubling.

When Jordan emerged from the principal's office, Nicholas pushed himself off the wall and trudged toward her. With his head down, she couldn't see his expression.

"We need to talk in the car." She didn't want others to overhear their conversation. She was determined to get to the bottom of what was happening to Nicholas.

Five minutes later with the air-conditioning cooling the interior of the car, Jordan sat behind the steering wheel in the parking lot of Key Elementary, Nicholas in the front seat next to her. "What's going on at school?"

"I don't understand the other guys' fascination with video games and football."

Well, neither did she but that didn't solve the problem her son had. He was more comfortable with adults. "Are they making fun of you?"

"I'm supposed to play dumb." Nicholas looked directly at her. "I can't do that. If some of them would do their homework, they could answer the teacher's questions. I'm bored and miserable."

"How about the enrichment class?"

"It meets twice a week for an hour. I need more. Randy was telling me about being schooled at home. May I try that? That way the class won't hold me back. I can learn at my own rate."

And going up another grade wasn't an option. "I'll think about it. I'll even go to the Helping Hands Homeschooling meeting tonight and see what they have to offer." Jordan pulled out of her parking space and headed to the street running in front of the school. "Because, Nicholas, I'll need help, and I want to make sure I can have opportunities for you to socialize if I homeschool you."

"I don't think like kids my age."

"You seem to like Randy, Jana and Ashley."

"Yeah, they're different."

Maybe if she could get Nicholas to socialize outside school, it would work better for her son. She was glad the HHH meeting was that evening, but she needed to know more before she committed to homeschooling. Was that the best option for her son? Could she provide him with the needed academics as well as opportunities to be with other kids?

Would Zachary be there? He'd said something about going because he was involved in the planning of an HHH Junior Rodeo Event at the ranch. She'd tried calling him several times since Saturday to set up a meeting with him, but each time she'd hung up before the phone had even rung once. The thought of seeing him that evening sent her pulse racing through her body. Should she even go?

When Jordan and Nicholas arrived at the Tallgrass Community Center where the Helping Hands Homeschooling group's meeting took place, the first person she saw was Zachary standing near his older sister, Becca.

"Mom, I see Randy. He told me to join him when I came."

"Fine." She couldn't take her eyes off Zachary.

He lifted his head and fastened his gaze on her. For a brief moment she was swept back to the time he'd approached her after a football game for the first time. Her heart reacted as it had then—tapping a fast staccato against her rib cage.

Something akin to that look they had exchanged all those years ago flickered into his eyes. Then suddenly he banked the fiery gleam. Even from across the large room she saw the tensing of his shoulders, the hardening of his jaw as though he gritted his teeth.

She tore her attention away. Not far from her, Alexa stood with a tall man who wore wire-rimmed glasses.

Plastering a smile on her face, Jordan headed for the young woman she'd met at the ranch. Maybe she could work her way toward Zachary and casually find out about his work schedule.

Because her mother was right. She couldn't postpone this discussion concerning Nicholas much longer. If she told him, she needed to do it soon. The longer she waited the more she would have to explain.

"It's great seeing you at the meeting. Are you thinking of homeschooling?" Alexa asked after introducing Ian to Jordan.

"I'm thinking about it. I wanted to find out what resources were available to someone like me who doesn't have any training in teaching."

"Dr. Nancy Baker, the founder of HHH, is a professor at Tallgrass Community College. She has a lot of materials and books available that you can access."

"Before you two talk shop, I see Zachary. I need to see him about the HHH Junior Rodeo Event. Nice meeting you." Ian nodded toward her, squeezed Alexa's hand, then weaved his way through the throng toward Zachary.

For a few seconds Jordan's gaze followed Ian's path until he reached Zachary, who caught her looking. She quickly averted her eyes. "I'd like to check into homeschooling. Nicholas isn't doing as well as he should at school right now. He's so bright, but his potential isn't being met. I'm not sure, though, I can do any better. He's been studying algebra on his own with some help from me, but it's been a while since I did it. I'm having a hard time keeping up."

"Ian is starting his second math group involving algebra for homeschoolers next week. We have a medical doctor in this group who teaches a different science course every three months—human anatomy starts in September, too.

Those courses are part of the co-op classes some of the kids tap into."

"So I don't have to teach every subject? Because there are a few I'm not good at."

"No one is. If you have some kind of expertise, you might want to offer a course for the group, but it's not a requirement."

"My job is a computer graphic designer. It might be fun doing something with that. I'll have to think about it."

"Let me introduce you to Nancy before the meeting begins." Alexa searched the large room. "Ah, I see her talking to Ian and Zachary." The young woman started for them.

Jordan braced herself with a deep breath and followed Alexa. Maybe no one else sensed the tension flowing from Zachary as she and Alexa joined the small group with Ian and Nancy, but Jordan did. That tic in Zachary's jawline jerked.

"This is Jordan, Nancy. She's thinking about home-schooling her son." Alexa stepped next to Ian, who slipped his arm around her shoulder.

Nancy shook Jordan's hand. "Great. If you need any help, there are plenty of us to ask."

"I wondered if I could come look at your materials. Nicholas needs a lot of enrichment, and I want to make sure I can give it to him." Jordan shifted from one foot to the other, conscious of Zachary next to her. Only inches from him, her arm prickled as though there was a physical connection.

"Fine. How about we set up a time to talk, and then you can look through the resources? Say tomorrow morning at eleven?"

"I appreciate that. I don't want the situation at school to go on too long."

"Then I'll see you at eleven. Now if you all will excuse me, I need to get this meeting started. We've got an HHH Junior Rodeo Event to plan for in October." Nancy walked toward the front of the room.

"What's going on at school?" Zachary's deep voice, with a husky edge, broke the momentary silence.

Suddenly Jordan faced him alone because Ian and Alexa moved off to sit in a row not far away. "He's teased a lot because he's smart. He has trouble socializing with some of the kids his age. But mainly Nicholas isn't being challenged enough in school." She didn't want to go into too much detail. That could lead to questions she wasn't prepared to answer.

He scanned the group of children filing into the room off the main one. "It looks like he's getting along great with Randy." He gestured toward Nicholas, who was laughing and talking with the boy as they trailed behind the group of kids. "I know that Randy wanted to learn to ride as much as your son did. Nicholas will be a good addition to the Saturday riding group. They both have a fascination with the rodeo."

"Nicholas said something to you about that?"

"Yes, he wanted me to teach him to ride a bronco."

"That's not gonna happen."

"He could learn some of the less risky activities like barrel racing."

Racing! Falling off a horse going fast! She ground her teeth and kept those thoughts to herself. As Nancy started the meeting, Jordan realized they were the only two not sitting. Two chairs nearby seemed the logical choice for them to sit in, but she didn't want to be seated next to Zachary. How in the world was she going to handle him being in Nicholas's life as his father?

Chapter Four

Why was he sitting next to Jordan at this meeting? The question needled Zachary with pinpricks of awareness of the woman who was only inches away from him. The hair on his arm near hers actually stood up as though at attention. He'd suffered through the past hour while the group planned the HHH Junior Rodeo activities scheduled to be at his ranch, but he'd hardly heard what had been said. The turmoil in his mind drowned out the voices. Worse, when he'd been called on to give his opinion, he'd barely been able to manage a coherent sentence in answer.

Since he saw her on Saturday, he hadn't been able to get the blonde dynamo out of his thoughts. She'd plagued his awakened moments and his sleep until exhaustion clung to him like sweat on a hard-ridden horse. She had no right to turn those dark brown eyes on him as though they hadn't parted ways after a nasty fight that had left him reeling eleven years ago. She'd been angry when she'd seen him in the corral a few days ago, as if he'd been the one who'd fled Tallgrass and hadn't looked back. He'd stayed around two months waiting for her to come to her senses. But not a word from her.

If his dream had been fulfilled, they would have been married, possibly with two or three kids by now. He hadn't wanted children right away, but he'd always wanted to be a father someday. But instead he'd decided to get as far away as possible from Tallgrass because of the constant reminders of what he and Jordan could have had.

After nine years he'd returned home, ready to put his life back together. He was through running from the home he'd loved and needed to put down roots. He was ready to complete one of his dreams—to own a ranch and raise horses, some of which were used in the rodeo. That was about the only way he was going to participate in the sport he'd loved after his injury in a bull trampling two years ago.

Suddenly, he noticed the people surrounding him and Jordan rising. The meeting was over? He blinked, wondering where the time had gone and what he'd agreed to as far as the HHH Junior Rodeo.

Zachary shot to his feet, needing to escape before Jordan totally befuddled him. He started to hurry away when her hand clamped on his arm and that tingling awareness became a flash through his body. Sweat beaded his brow. She'd always had that effect on him.

"I need to talk to you. Can we get together sometime soon?"

Her question threw him off-kilter. Talk to him? Get together? Why? He wanted to stay far away from her until he could tamp down the lingering feelings he had for her. Because being rejected by her once was enough. "I'm busy." For a second his gaze clung to her full lips—lips that he'd one time loved to kiss.

"This is important."

He dragged his focus to her chocolate-brown eyes, concern in their depths that tried to wheedle its way into his heart. "Is this about Nicholas?"

She blinked, her face going white. "Yes, how did you know?"

"Let me assure you I meant what I said on Saturday. He can still take riding lessons even if you don't decide to join this group. I don't go back on my word." Realizing she still clasped his arm, he shook it free. "Now, if you'll excuse me, I've got to go."

"But…"

He didn't wait for her to say anything else. Quickening his step, he escaped outside and drew in deep breaths of the hot summer air. The light breeze cooled his cheeks.

Nicholas. The boy's name flitted through his mind. She'd moved on without him, had another man's son— loved another man. He'd tried to move on and for a short time had even become engaged to a girl after he'd been on the rodeo circuit a few years. After his bull riding accident, she'd left him. Audrey had wanted to have children, and he wouldn't be able to give her any. No, he'd decided not feeling anything was so much better for him. He had his ranch and was doing what he loved to do, raising horses. That was his life now, and he wasn't going to let Jordan's return change his plans nor the memories of their good times together.

Jordan looked up from working on her laptop to see her sister come into the kitchen. "Have you been hiding from me?" She clasped the edge of the table.

Rachel poured herself some coffee and sank into the chair next to Jordan. "Granny told me I'd better come down or you were going to send out a search party."

"Yeah, I have a beef with you. You sent me to Zachary's ranch last Saturday and now I'm stuck taking Nicholas there tomorrow. What were you thinking?" She couldn't keep her rising ire from resonating in her voice.

"That you two needed to work the past out."

"Have I interfered with your life?" Rachel had never been able to resist meddling.

"Only because you've been in South Carolina until four weeks ago. In time you'll be right in the middle like you were as a child."

"Me? Telling you what you should do? You've always done that. Don't. I can live my own life now." The words exploded from Jordan's mouth like compressed soda in a shaken bottle.

"I'll always care about you. I can't stop being your big sis."

"Sister, not mother."

Rachel's gaze connected with Jordan's. "I'm sorry."

Her apology deflated Jordan's annoyance. She couldn't stay mad at her sister for long. Growing up, Rachel had protected her. She'd listened to her. She'd been there through the pain of her breakup. "I know," she murmured, her tone a ragged stream.

Rachel took a sip from her mug. "Hmm. Your coffee is so much better than Mom's."

"How do you know I made that?" After Jordan closed down the program she was working on, she pushed her laptop to the side and lifted her mug to take a drink.

"Because you got Granny's cooking genes. Mom didn't. I didn't."

"Speaking of Granny, who is this Doug person?"

"A sweet man who is seventy and taken with our grandmother."

"Seventy! She's robbing the cradle."

Rachel raised her forefinger to her lips. "Shh. Don't

let her hear you say that. She'll probably outlast Doug by years."

She wished she were as together as her sister or Granny. "Rachel, I need help. What am I gonna do?"

"Tell Zachary about Nicholas?"

"Do you know what that will do to me?" Jordan bit down on her thumbnail, then suddenly realized she'd reverted to a bad habit and said, "See what I'm doing just thinking about the havoc that will cause in my life. It took me years to break myself of biting my fingernails. Now I'm doing it again. Home less than a month."

"Zachary has a right to know whether he wants to be in Nicholas's life or not. It's his choice. Not yours. I told you years ago that you needed to get in touch with him."

"I know I need to do it. I just don't know how. I can't march up to him and say 'Nicholas is your son.'"

Rachel winced. "No, you need to cushion the news a little."

"Like you did when you told me Zachary owned the ranch?" The urge to chew on her fingernails inundated her. Jordan sat on her hands instead.

"Just do it. The longer you think about it the more upset you're going to be. Quit analyzing the problem to death."

"I can't change who I am."

"Oh, but you have. You used to take risks. Now you think everything to death."

"Yeah, well, finding out you're pregnant with a child whose father doesn't want to have anything to do with you can go a long way to curing you of taking risks."

Rising, Rachel finished her last swallow of coffee and strolled to the sink to set her mug in it. "I'm going back into hiding. Let me know when you tell him."

"*If* I tell him," Jordan couldn't resist saying to her older sister's back as she left the room.

* * *

Jordan slid into the pew at the Tallgrass Community Church between Nicholas and her sister.

"I'm glad you could make it," Rachel whispered.

She smiled sweetly at her only sibling. "With the move I've been swamped, but I'm working to strengthen my faith. I'll admit I let life interfere in South Carolina."

"Did you tell him yesterday when you went to the ranch for Nicholas's lesson?"

With a glance at her son, she bent toward Rachel and lowered her voice to the barest level. "No and don't bring it up."

At that moment the music began to play, signaling the service would begin in a few minutes. Jordan bowed her head and folded her hands together in her lap.

Lord, I'm here like I promised, but I'm still clueless what to do. Yesterday I couldn't have gotten the words out to say anything to Zachary if my life depended on it. Where do I start? How do I do it? Please help me. Amen.

A commotion behind her drew her attention. First Becca then Ashley, Mike and Cal entered the pew. Next came Becca's husband, Paul, with Zachary on the end, right behind Nicholas.

Her son twisted around and grinned at Zachary, waving his hand. "Howdy."

Howdy? Her son had never said that word in his whole life. She groaned and kept her gaze focused straight ahead. But the hairs on her nape tingled.

"Mom, Zachary is behind us."

Every nerve ending was acutely aware of that fact. "Shh, hon. Church is about to start." Which thankfully it did with the choir marching in singing "Onward, Christian Soldiers."

Zachary rose as the rest of the congregation did to sing

the opening hymn, but he could hardly concentrate on the words of the song. Not with Jordan standing within arm's length of him. So close he could tug her into an embrace. That thought sent panic coursing through him. He should have expected her to show up at church with her family attending the same one as he did and prepared himself better—hardened his defenses against Jordan, who had always managed to get under his skin like a burr in a saddle blanket.

After seeing Jordan with Nicholas yesterday at his ranch, he didn't know if he could continue teaching her son how to ride. The boy reminded him of Jordan. He liked him a lot—probably too much.

When he looked at Nicholas, all he could think about was the child he never would have. The boy should have been his with Jordan. That had been his plan all those years ago. They would marry. He would make his living on the rodeo circuit until he had enough money for a ranch. Then they could start a family. He had his ranch thanks to a fruitful career on the rodeo circuit for five years. But now he couldn't have any kids—not since the accident in the National Finals in bull riding. It had left him lame and unable to father the children he'd always wanted.

He sat again after the song, his hands clenched at his sides. There were a few days imprinted in his mind forever—when he first met Jordan, when they broke up and when he'd nearly died in the ring, riding a two-thousand-pound bull.

The longer he stayed in the pew behind Jordan the tenser he became. When the service ended an hour later, his muscles ached like they did when he was trying to rein in an untrained horse.

Nicholas turned toward him. "I didn't know you go to this church. That's neat. I had a great time yesterday."

"I'm glad. Before long you're gonna be riding rings around the others." There was no way he couldn't teach the boy how to ride. He had to find a way to stay away from Jordan and still help Nicholas. But he was beginning to think that would be impossible.

Nicholas beamed. "I want to be the best."

Jordan angled toward her son. "The best what?"

"Rider. I hope to participate in barrel racing at the HHH Junior Rodeo."

Jordan's eyes grew round. "You do?" Then her mouth firmed into a thin line.

"Yes. If I'm good, Mom, then you won't worry about me."

"Hey, Nicholas, want to join us?" Randy called from the aisle.

"Okay, Mom?"

"Fine. We'll be in the rec hall," Jordan said while the rest of her family filed out the other end of the pew.

Leaving Zachary practically alone with Jordan. Even his own family had abandoned him. He faced her, the muscles in his neck tightening even more than before until he didn't know if he could speak, which reminded him of the time years ago when they had first talked. He'd been sweaty, tired and tongue-tied, but he'd needed to make sure she was okay after her fall while cheerleading at the game.

"All the way home yesterday Nicholas couldn't stop talking about his lesson. I wish I had stayed to watch it. I had an errand to run, but I'll stay next week."

"Don't," slipped out of his mouth before he could stop the word.

Her forehead creased. "What do you mean?"

"I think the less we're around each other the better it is. Let's face it. The time when we were friends is past. You go your way. I'll go mine." There was a part of him—a desperate part that couldn't believe he was saying that to her. But it was true. Their time together was in the past.

"But Nicholas—"

"He's a joy to teach. He's welcome to come for the riding lessons. But I want you to drop him off and come back to pick him up." Because if she stood around watching, that would be all he would focus on. And he needed to concentrate on working with the kids, not on Jordan. She distracted him more than he wished. "Now if you'll excuse me, I need to find my family."

Striding away before she wanted to talk more, he scanned the near-empty sanctuary, surprised that most of the churchgoers had left. That was Jordan's effect on him. She had the ability to wipe away his common sense. He could still remember that time years ago when he had been competing at a rodeo and Jordan had been late arriving to watch him. When he saw her sit in the stands, he kept his attention on her a few seconds longer than he should have. He ended up on the ground, his arm broken, berating himself for losing his concentration. He wouldn't let her get close enough to do that again. Too dangerous.

On the following Tuesday Jordan parked in front of the barn in nearly the same place as she had on Saturday for her son's second riding lesson. This time Nicholas wasn't with her. This time she was on a mission: to find Zachary, get him alone and tell him about his son.

She knew she had to and waiting would only make it worse. Knots riddled her stomach, and she hadn't eaten much in the past twenty-four hours. For a moment at church on Sunday, she'd contemplated telling him then, but he'd hightailed it out of the sanctuary so fast she hadn't had a chance. It probably hadn't been the best place anyway. They needed to be totally alone.

She saw the same black pickup as she had Saturday. She hoped that meant he was inside. Trudging toward the entrance, she surveyed the ranch. Several corrals with some horses surrounded the black barn. A little farther away were green pastures with groups of horses, some with colts and fillies. His place had a well-tended look about it, which didn't surprise her because that was the kind of person she'd known as a teenager. He took care of his own.

Inside, the hay-scented air cooled a couple of degrees. She peered down the long center of the cavernous structure with stalls on each side. "Zachary," she called out.

A short wrangler stuck his head out of an open door. "You just missed him. He's at his house."

"The blue one by the road?"

"No, ma'am. He lives due west. A small white place. You can't miss it if you stay on the dirt road that runs in front of here."

She smiled although the corners of her mouth quivered. "Thanks." Seeing him at his house would be perfect. They could talk without being disturbed.

A few minutes later, she pulled up to a one-story white house, again well tended with a small vegetable garden to the left and a flower bed running the length of its front. Exiting her car, she inhaled a calming breath, full of the scent of the recently mowed grass. A swing hung from the ceiling of the wraparound porch, offering a comfortable haven at the end of the day. A sense of peace enveloped her as she took in her surroundings.

That peace was shattered a few seconds later when the front door opened and Zachary emerged from his house with a scowl on his face. She stiffened. The carefully prepared speech she'd rehearsed for hours wiped completely from her mind as he descended the steps and strode across the lawn toward her. His features were schooled in a neutral expression.

"What brings you out here?" His voice remained flat like the prairie around them.

Seeing him suddenly made her want to postpone telling him. Forever. The muscles in her throat convulsed. She backed up a few steps until she bumped into her car behind her and she couldn't go anywhere else. Trapped.

I need to leave. How could they work together for Nicholas's benefit? "I have to talk to you."

"What do you want?"

"A glass of water."

His brow crinkled. "What?"

"Water. I'm thirsty." Anything to delay what she needed to do.

"You came all the way out here for water?" He threaded his fingers through his hair.

"No, but I could use some first."

Several heartbeats later he shrugged. "Suit yourself." He spun on his heel and marched toward his place.

Jordan fortified herself with another deep breath and trailed after him.

He banged into the house, closing the door on her.

The barrier didn't bode well for the conversation she had to have with him. She sought the comfort of the porch swing and sat. *Lord, I need your help. Please give me the right words to say to him.*

The door opened, and Zachary came outside holding a tall glass with ice water in it. He handed it to her then lounged against the white railing and folded his arms over his chest.

Her hand trembling, she sipped several gulps of the cold water although it did nothing to alleviate the tightness in her throat. "Thank you. That hit the spot."

His biceps bunched. "Why did you come all the way out here, Jordan? What's going on?"

"I needed to talk to you in private. I thought this might be a good place and time."

His jaw clenched. "For?" He crossed his legs, totally closing himself off to her.

Her heart pounded so fast and loud she wondered if he heard it. Perspiration broke out on her forehead, upper lips and her palms. "Nicholas…" Her son's name came out in a whispered rush, the air sucked out of her lungs.

"Is this about homeschooling? I don't know anything about that. Talk with Becca if you want. She could answer your questions."

She put the glass on a table near the swing before she dropped it, then ran her damp palms on her capri jeans. Her chest rose and fell with the deep inhalation. "No, I went by and talked with Dr. Baker last Thursday. I've decided to take him out of school and teach him at home. I've got to do something different because what he's doing now isn't working." The sense of doom and the sensation of being cornered besieged her as though she were under attack.

"Then what is it?"

Tell him. Before you lose your nerve. "Nicholas—" The blood rushed into her ears. She gripped the edge of the swing, her fingernails digging into the wood, her breath trapped in her lungs. "Nicholas loves coming out here, and I want to thank you again for giving him lessons."

A sigh blew out between pursed lips. "What is it you're avoiding? This isn't like you not to come to…" His gaze latched onto hers. She could almost see the wheels turning in his head. He shoved away from the railing, not one emotion on his face. "How old is Nicholas?"

"He turned ten in April. He's small for his age. He was born a month early. Nicholas is your son."

He slumped back against the wooden post, clutching it. The dark stubble of his beard accentuated a gray pallor. His eyes fluttered. A flush of excitement glimmered in his expression. But quickly joy morphed into a bitter twist like a bundle of barbed wire. "You kept my son from me?"

She nodded slowly—all words lumped together into a huge knot in her throat.

His gaze clashed with hers. He opened his mouth to say more but snapped it closed, his teeth clicking from the force. Pivoting away, he clamped his hands on the railing and leaned into it. With his shoulders slumped forward, he dropped his head.

She collapsed back against the swing, twisting her hands together in her lap. She should have eased into the news. Cushioned the blow. But it wouldn't have really made a difference. It wouldn't change the fact Nicholas was his son.

Finally he turned slowly toward her. The painful look in his eyes tore down all her reasons for never telling him and made a mockery of the hurt she'd experienced at him not contacting her. Then a shutter fell over his face. He wore a cold mask as though they were strangers—adversaries, and she supposed they were now.

"Why didn't you tell me this eleven years ago? Even a week ago?"

The lethal quiet of his words sent a chill down her spine. He wasn't innocent in this whole affair. She'd given him two chances, and he'd ignored her—hurt her and left her to deal with Nicholas's birth and illness by herself. She'd learned the hard way to rely only on herself and God. No one else. Certainly not him.

"I called you and left several messages. You never called back."

He fisted his hands. "I never received any messages from you."

"But I talked with your sister once, then later when I called again, to your mother. I asked her to have you call me. That it was important. In spite of the fact she informed me that you were engaged and happy, I was going to tell you I would be having a baby within two months. Your child." For a few seconds the memory hurled her back in time. A bone-deep ache overpowered her.

"I dated some but nothing serious. I didn't get engaged until after I left the army."

"Then I would have a talk with your mother." Her anger seeded itself in her heart, and she bolted to her feet. "I'm not the villain here. I tried. I decided while I was having Nicholas three weeks after that call that I would never force a man—you—to be his father."

He uncurled his hands then curled them again. Taking two steps, he cut the distance between them and thrust his face close to hers. "After calling twice, *you* decided I didn't have a right to know I had a child. That I couldn't be his father. Who are you to make that decision for me?"

"I'm Nicholas's mother. I'm the person you told that if I left Tallgrass that it was over between us. I'm the one who stayed in the hospital chapel on my knees praying to God to let my son live when he was struggling to stay alive. It was your mother who took pleasure in telling me you had a new woman in your life."

"Leave. You've done what you came to do."

He stalked to the front door and yanked it open. The sound of it slamming shut reverberated through the air. Jordan stared at the barrier between her and Zachary, her brief fury deflating. He had a right to be angry. But so did she. Why hadn't his mother told him?

She started to knock on his door, stopped and decided to

leave as he asked. Emotionally she didn't have the energy to talk to him anymore. She still needed to tell Nicholas. Tonight when her mother took Granny to church. Nicholas and she would have the house to themselves. She hurried toward her car to put as much distance between her and Zachary as possible. Maybe then the pain would go away.

Numb, Zachary stood in the middle of his living room, staring at the floor as though that would help him to understand what had just happened. His mind swirled like a dust devil on the prairie. He couldn't grasp a thought beyond he had a son. Nicholas.

How could Jordan keep something that important from him? He sank into the chair next to the phone, his legs weak, his heart hammering so hard it hurt.

And his mother had kept Jordan's call from him. He flinched at the double whammy. If only he'd known about Nicholas, everything would be different.

No, he couldn't change what Jordan had done all those years ago, but he needed to know the truth. His hands shook as he reached for the phone to call his mother, who now lived in Arizona. He had to hear from her that she had kept Jordan's phone call from him. Even if his mom had, it didn't excuse Jordan. He hesitated with the last number. What good would it do to know his mother had kept a secret from him? He loved his parents, hated for anything to come between them. And yet, she'd had no right.

He moved the receiver toward its cradle. He halted in midair. No, he needed the truth—all of it. Then he would deal with the fact he had a son, that between Jordan and his mother he'd lost over ten years with his child. A child he'd dreamed of having but with the rodeo accident had been wrenched from his grasp. Was this a second chance? He pressed the last number.

When his mother answered, his tight grip on the phone shot pain down his arm. "Jordan Masterson has returned to Tallgrass. She just left here. She told me she asked you to have me call her that spring after we broke up. Did she?"

"Becca told me she was back home, that you two have seen each other several times."

"Mom, did she leave a message for me?" His heartbeat thundered in his ears as though a storm crashed against his skull.

"She called in March. You'd just finished boot camp and had been sent overseas. You talked about having met a girl you liked and had even gone out on a few dates. I didn't want you to be hurt again by Jordan so I didn't tell you."

He clamped his teeth together and watched the second hand make half a circle on the kitchen clock before saying, "That wasn't your decision to make." Somehow his voice only held a hint of the turmoil he was experiencing.

"That was more than ten years ago. Why are you bringing it up now?"

"Because Jordan just told me I have a son." A son! His insides felt as though a tornado raged within him.

The sound of a swift intake of air followed by a long silence greeted Zachary. He collapsed into the chair at his round oak table, holding the phone in one hand while kneading his temple with the other. He was ecstatic; he was angry.

"Are you sure he's your son?"

His mother's question sucker punched him. Pain radiated throughout his body as the fact he was a father finally sank into his brain. Really. Thinking back to what Nicholas looked like—the same eyes and set of his chin with a cleft—Zachary closed his eyes. How could he have missed it? "Yes, Mom, Nicholas is my son." *I have a son after all these years.*

"I have another grandchild? How could she keep something like that from you, from our family?"

"She called right before he was born to let me know she was pregnant." Part of him wanted to take back his defense of Jordan, but there were so many good memories tangled up in the bad ones that he couldn't totally put the blame on her.

"She should have said something to me. I'd have told you if she had mentioned she was having your child."

The accusatory tone sliced across his chest, a band drawn taut. "She said something about you telling her I was engaged. I guess that stopped her."

"Oh, that." His mother sighed. "That still doesn't excuse her for not saying something to you."

No, it doesn't. She should have called back. Everything would have been different if she had.

"She was wrong, son."

A long, long silence stalked her last words. He shifted in the chair.

"I'm so sorry I didn't say anything. I didn't want you to get hurt again. I don't know what else to say."

The anger he felt toward Jordan eclipsed any he could have toward his mother. Jordan should have called and called until she had spoken to him personally. How could he ever trust her again? How could he forgive her for stealing ten years of being a father from him?

Jordan downed the last swallow of her fifth cup of coffee in the past two hours. She had to tell Nicholas as soon as her mother and grandmother left for church. After her encounter with Zachary today, she couldn't put it off any longer.

Her grandmother shuffled into the room, wearing a pink chiffon dress, with makeup on her face, and her short gray hair done in soft curls.

"You look great. What's the occasion?" Jordan rose and started to help Granny into the chair she'd been sitting in.

Her grandmother shook off her assistance. "Child, I wish you would stop listening to your mother. I can manage by myself." She sank into the chair and waved Jordan toward the one next to her. "Doug's going to be at the Prairie Pride meeting tonight. I finally talked him into being part of the group at church."

"You really like him?"

A twinkle entered her eyes, and her mouth tilted up in a huge grin. "Yeah. And I don't care what Eileen thinks."

"Mom will come around. Give her time."

"Time isn't my friend. I'm going to grasp the brass ring while I can still reach for it."

Jordan chuckled. "I love you. After the day I've had, you still manage to make me laugh."

"You finally told your young man about Nicholas? I know you've been praying about it."

She chewed on a fingernail then realized what she was doing and dropped her hand into her lap, grasping both of them together to keep from doing it. "Zachary isn't my young man, but yes I did today." Seeing him earlier had renewed feelings she wanted—needed—to deny, especially when she discovered that Zachary hadn't known about the calls all those years ago.

"I imagine he wasn't too pleased."

"That's putting it mildly."

"And now you need to talk with Nicholas?"

Jordan nodded. "I've made a mess of everything. I wish I'd never run into Zachary." At least a part of her wished that, but another part wondered if she and Zachary could put the past behind them and start over.

Her grandmother cocked her head and studied Jordan with those sensitive dark eyes that could see right through her. "Do you really? You don't think this is for the best in the end?"

Her clasped hands squeezed until her fingers tingled. "You always did like Zachary."

"He's a likeable young man. But what I feel isn't the point. This is about Nicholas and you, and your son deserves to know."

Jordan dropped her head and stared at her hands twisting together. "I'm afraid I'm gonna have to get used to seeing Zachary."

"Good. It's about time. I hated seeing you two break up."

Jordan looked at her grandmother. "You never said anything before. You sound like Rachel."

"It was your mistake to make."

"Mistake? It wouldn't have worked back then. I wanted different things than Zachary."

"How about now?"

"I don't know him. I realized that when I saw him."

Jordan's mom came into the kitchen. "There you are. We need to get going or you'll be late."

"And we wouldn't want that." Her grandmother winked at Jordan then rose slowly, peering at her. "I suggest you get to know him."

"I was looking for your walker. Where is it?" Eileen scanned the room.

"I put it away."

"You can't."

"I can do what I want. I don't need it." Her grandmother hobbled toward the back door, saying, "Let's get going. I don't want to be late," then disappeared outside.

Her mom huffed and stalked past Jordan. "See what I have to put up with."

"See you in a couple hours."

Jordan pushed to her feet and took her mug to the sink. For a few seconds the dark out the window enticed her attention. Anything to prolong going to Nicholas's room. Anything to prolong having the conversation about his father. Anything to rewrite the past. Not possible. A long breath hissed from her lips.

She moved toward the hallway. The doorbell rang. She quickly diverted her path to the front foyer, eager for the interruption. She swung the door open. All eagerness vanished.

Zachary stood in the entrance. His commanding presence stole her breath and her thoughts.

Chapter Five

"What are you doing here?" Stepping out onto the porch, Jordan closed the door behind her. Blocking the entrance to the house, she faced Zachary, his expression totally closed.

"I'm here to see my son."

"You can't. I haven't…" Panic choked off her words.

He moved closer. "I'm not leaving until I see Nicholas."

She backed up. "I haven't talked with him yet."

"Good." Taking another stride, Zachary stood in front of her, invading her personal space. "I want to be there when you tell him. I'm his father."

"No!"

A tic in his jawline was the only sign he didn't like her answer.

The slashing line of his mouth underscored his anger. "Jordan, I want to be in my son's life. I think you at least owe me that."

"I know my son. You don't. I can't—"

"The only reason I don't know Nicholas is because you didn't tell me I had a son. I want to change that. I've lost ten years with him. I'm not losing another day." He thrust his face close.

The scent of his peppermint toothpaste taunted her, sparking a vivid memory of the first time he'd kissed her. She slammed the lid quickly on that thought. She needed all her wits about her. Squaring her shoulders, she met his pinpoint gaze. "He's also my son."

His lips pressed together. "I want to be with you when you tell him."

A constriction about her chest pulled tight. She grappled for something to say, but all she could think of was he was Nicholas's father. She was no longer the only one in her son's life. She would have to share him with Zachary. This was exactly what she'd been afraid would happen. "Fine." She drew in a composing breath. "But I'm the one who tells him."

With a nod, he backed away several steps.

Jordan took another deep breath, trying to fill her oxygen-deprived lungs. Pivoting away from Zachary, she fumbled for the handle then shoved the door open. As she crossed the foyer toward the stairs, she slung a look over her shoulder. He hung back for a few seconds, surveying her home.

His harsh gaze returned to hers. "At least some things haven't changed." He strode toward her.

This was the house she'd grown up in, and Zachary knew this house. He'd spent a lot of time here while they had been dating in high school. "If my mother has a say in it, they will. She wants to redo the whole place."

"Where are your mother and grandmother?"

"They're at church. They won't be back for a few hours." She mounted the steps, feeling Zachary's eyes on her back.

The walk down the hallway to Nicholas's room took

seconds, but all she could think about was the eternity she'd endured during her son's heart operation while she waited to hear from the surgeon. The same empty feeling in her stomach. The same chill blanketing her. The same numbness as if what she was experiencing wasn't real.

At Nicholas's door, she knocked then pushed it open. Her son sat at his desk in front of his computer.

He twisted toward her, an excited smile on his face. "Mom, I figured out this problem." He tapped the screen. His attention shifted to Zachary, who appeared behind Jordan. "Hi, Zachary. What are you doing here?"

The very same question she'd demanded only ten minutes ago. "We have something to talk to you about," she said, not wanting Zachary to answer.

"Is it about the riding lessons?"

"No, hon." She moved into the room and sat on Nicholas's bed before her legs gave out.

"Oh. What's wrong?" Nicholas scooted around to face her, but his gaze strayed to Zachary for a few seconds before returning to her.

"Nothing is really wrong." *Who am I kidding? Everything is wrong.* The words she needed to say stuck in her throat, burning a hole. She swallowed once. Twice.

Zachary stepped toward Nicholas.

"Mom?" His eyebrows slashed down.

"Remember when I told you that your dad didn't want to be involved in your life?"

Nicholas nodded.

"Well, I was wrong. He does." A fortifying breath did little to fill her lungs. Zachary opened his mouth. Alarm dislodged her clogged words, and she blurted out, "Zachary is your father."

Nicholas's jaw dropped. He peered at her for a brief

moment, then fastened his stare on Zachary. "You are? Why didn't you say something when I was at the ranch?"

Zachary spread his arms wide, palms outward. "I—I didn't—"

"He didn't know." When Nicholas looked at her again, her stomach clenched into a hard ball.

Nicholas's confusion ripped her composure. She wanted to hug him. To hold him in her arms until everything was back to normal. To soothe his turmoil until the shadows faded from his eyes.

She'd handled this all wrong. She should have told her son first by herself no matter what Zachary had insisted. The minute he'd entered the picture all the carefully planned words she'd rehearsed evaporated like water in Death Valley. "I never told Zachary about you."

The furrows in her child's forehead deepened. "Why not?"

She threw a glance at Zachary, catching the same question in his eyes. "I tried. I called him several times to tell him, but he wasn't there and he never returned my calls." All of a sudden, even to her own ears, the reason wasn't strong enough. "I was nineteen. Hurt he hadn't called me back. I..." She couldn't tell her son it was pride that had kept her from trying to get in touch with Zachary again. Pride and fear of rejection.

"I never received the messages to call your mother. Through a series of unfortunate incidents, not your mom's fault, I didn't discover you were my son until today when she told me."

Surprise flitted through her. *Not my fault?* That wasn't what he'd implied earlier.

Zachary covered the few feet between him and his son. "That's why I'm here tonight. We have a lot to catch up on.

It looks like you're working on algebra. I didn't do algebra until I was fourteen."

Nicholas studied Zachary's face for a long moment. "We look alike. I should have seen it."

"If you aren't looking for it, you wouldn't notice." Zachary returned his son's intense survey. "But you're right. We have similar features." He sat on the long chest at the end of the bed, his legs spread, his elbows on his thighs, his hands loosely clasped. "Tell me about what you're doing on the computer."

With a narrowed gaze thrown her way, Nicholas scooted his chair over a few inches to give Zachary a better view of the screen. Then her son launched into his plan to have calculus mastered by the age of fourteen. She prayed that Nicholas would talk to her about what he was feeling after Zachary left, but if that glance was any indication she was in for a rough night with her son.

After listening to the boy's explanation of what he wanted to study, Zachary examined Nicholas's—no, scratch that, his son's—bedroom. It was nothing like his when he was growing up. On a wall was a detailed map of the solar system while on the opposite one was a map of the world with red and blue pins stuck in it—probably at least fifty. Another poster listed the periodic table. The full double bookcases next to his desk held volumes of books that an adult would have—not a child of ten. When he skimmed over the other titles, his gaze lighting upon *War and Peace,* questions flooded Zachary's mind. How smart was his child? How was he gonna relate to him? The fact he'd missed the first ten years struck him like a punch to the gut. He was out of step with his son and didn't know if they would ever have anything in common. His one chance to be a father.

"So you really enjoy math?" He'd hated the subject in school.

"Yes, sir. It comes easy to me."

Zachary heard the creak of the bed as Jordan stood. He slipped a look toward her, hoping she would leave him alone with Nicholas, but she remained nearby. The feel of her gaze on him made him clutch his hands together. "What don't you like?"

"Really not much. I guess writing. But I love to read, especially history and biographies. You can learn so much when you read about a famous person."

"What was the last book you read?" Zachary couldn't remember the last one he'd read—had to be years ago.

"A six-volume series by Winston Churchill concerning World War II. Next I want to read about Hitler to get a better sense of what happened at that time."

Zachary's mouth hung open. Quickly he snapped it closed. *I should have seen the resemblance. Figured it out. But I never thought Jordan would keep something like that from me.* The anger, just below the surface, surged to the foreground along with self-doubt. *I'm so not prepared to be a father.*

"I find it's necessary to read both sides of an issue or topic. Don't you think?"

"Yeah. What about you, Jordan?" Zachary swung his attention toward the woman who'd not readied him for this moment. He'd enjoyed history in school while Jordan hadn't. Maybe he could find a common bond with his son after all. He could go to the bookstore, find some books on World War II.

"Sure, both sides are important."

The uncomfortable look on her face didn't vindicate him. For his son's sake he would be tied to Jordan, and he needed to make this work, somehow.

"Mom, what are we having for dinner?"

"Dinner? Uh…" Her mouth twisted as she shot a glance toward the door. "I guess I can fix some sandwiches."

"Will you stay for dinner?" His son clicked off the computer.

Zachary didn't know if he could sit at a table with Jordan and act as if everything would be okay. It wouldn't be. And yet the eagerness in Nicholas's expression prompted him to say, "Yeah, that sounds nice."

"Fine. Why don't you come help me?" Jordan stared right at Zachary.

"My idea of fixing a meal is opening a can of soup."

She blew a breath out, her gaze darting between Zachary and the doorway. "It shouldn't take me five minutes. Nicholas, make sure you wash up."

After she hurried from the room, Nicholas checked his watch. "She'll probably have it done in four."

"Why do you say that?" Zachary asked, amused for the first time that day.

"She's afraid to leave us alone."

"Very perceptive."

"Not really. She's just very obvious. What happened with you and Mom?"

It was his turn to squirm. "You don't pull any punches. How old are you?" He knew, but the question just slipped out because the more he was around his son the older he seemed.

"Ten but sometimes I feel a lot older. I was sick a lot when I was younger and I spent a lot of time reading books. At least with them I could go places, do things I couldn't otherwise. That's what those pins on the map represent. Blue are my first choices of where I want to go. Red are the back-up ones."

Suddenly Zachary looked hard at his son. He hadn't had

a chance to be a boy. Maybe that was what he could do for his son. Teach him to play, have fun. "Then maybe I can do something about that. You said something about being interested in the rodeo."

His face brightening, Nicholas straightened. "Yes. I've read some books about it."

"Books are good, but experiencing it firsthand is so much better. I started participating in rodeo events for kids when I was your age. Actually earlier."

"Then I could, too."

Zachary wanted to say yes—should have the right to since he was the child's father—but caution made him murmur, "We'll have to run it by your mother first."

His son frowned. "She'll never let me. She gets scared that I'll get sick or hurt myself."

"The first thing you need to do is learn to ride well. Then we'll see after that."

"Nicholas, dinner is ready," Jordan shouted as if she stood at the bottom of the stairs.

"Let's go wash up, partner." Zachary rose. "I hear your mom is gonna teach you at home."

"Yeah, tomorrow is my last day at school and I'm so glad. It takes Mom a while to make up her mind." His son lowered his voice and bent closer. "She doesn't like change."

He settled a hand on his son's shoulder as they headed for the bathroom. "What's been going on at school?"

Nicholas shrugged. "Just the usual."

In the hallway Zachary faced the boy. "Are you being teased?"

He hung his head. "Yes. I don't fit in. I don't understand them. Today I was the last one to be picked for a team. That happens all the time. Then another kid laughed in class when I had to write an answer on the board."

Nicholas's injured tone magnified Zachary's anger at Jordan. "Why?" He could have been there to help his son—if only he'd known about him.

"My handwriting isn't legible. I've tried to make it better, but my fine motor skills aren't good."

Would he ever not be amazed what came out of his son's mouth? Nicholas was nothing like his niece and nephews. Zachary lifted his son's chin. "You have nothing to be ashamed about. You're smart. You have a lot to offer a friend." He started again toward the bathroom. "I can help you with that."

The dinner had been a disaster. Jordan carried the plates to the sink while Nicholas snagged Zachary and took him outside to show him his telescope. She'd wanted to follow, but after being excluded through most of the meal, it was obvious her son only wanted to spend time with his father.

During the meal Zachary and Nicholas had talked horses and riding, leaving her out of the conversation. What if she hadn't gone to the ranch that Saturday? Or come back to Tallgrass? Then she wouldn't be facing this problem. But remembering Nicholas's joy-filled expression and his laughter during the dinner made her realize telling Zachary had been for the best.

She sank into a chair at the kitchen table, placed her elbow on its top and cupped her chin. Tapping her finger against her cheek, she visualized Nicholas on the back of a horse, racing across the meadow. The next image of him flying over the animal's head and crashing into the hard ground sent alarm through her.

She bolted to her feet and marched to the back door. She was joining them whether they liked it or not. He was her son, too. She'd been his parent for the past ten years and wasn't going to turn the reins over to Zachary just because she'd made a mistake and hadn't told him about Nicholas.

Because now she realized she'd been totally wrong not to. Somehow she had to make sure that Zachary understood she regretted the decision she made all those years ago. That they should work together.

She flung open the door and stepped out onto the deck. Both Zachary and Nicholas glanced toward her then her son returned to showing Zachary how to adjust the telescope— one she'd spent a bonus on to get her son two Christmases ago. At the time the telescope had been taller than Nicholas. He spent hours outside watching the sky at night. He was determined to discover something new, and if she knew her son, he probably would one day.

"What are you all looking at?"

Zachary peered at her. "The rings of Saturn. I can't believe I'm actually seeing them."

She recalled the first time she'd seen them or the craters on the moon or Mars. "Yeah. They're neat." She watched father and son, and her heart expanded against her rib cage. She still needed to talk with Nicholas without Zachary around, but looking at them together firmed the rightness of her decision. "It's getting close to your bedtime."

"Ah, Mom."

"You've got to get up early for school. I'm sure you and Zachary will spend a lot of time together in the future. You need to take your bath—"

In the dim light from the kitchen, Nicholas pivoted, his arms straight at his sides, his hands balled. "I want to spend time with him *now*."

Stunned by the angrily spoken word, Jordan took a step back. "Nicholas."

"Partner, I need to leave, but why don't you and your

mother come out to the ranch tomorrow after school. I want to introduce you to my sister and her family. You've already met Ashley, but I have two nephews, too." Zachary stood behind her son—their son—his face in the shadows.

"But—but…" spluttered out of Nicholas's mouth before he closed it and stalked toward the door. Its slamming vibrated through the clear night air.

Jordan flinched, her eyes shutting as she scrubbed her hands down her face.

"Do you blame him?"

Zachary's quiet question chipped away at what composure she had left. "I blame you for not letting me prepare him for the news."

"Oh, I see. I was supposed to wait some more time to get to know *my* son while you come up with a way to explain why you never told me or him about who I am. Let's face it. There's no easy way to tell him you kept the truth from him and me."

Anger and guilt tangled together to form a knot in her throat. And now she had to deal with the consequences of that decision. How could she have thought that she could come home and continue merrily along with her life as she had for twenty-nine years? Because she hadn't known Zachary was in Tallgrass.

"I'm going, but I want my family to get to know Nicholas. He wants to come to the ranch tomorrow and meet them."

"If *your* family had given you my messages all those years ago, we wouldn't be standing here like this." She'd been wrong—but not the only one.

He drilled a look through her. "Touché. I'll give you that, but it still doesn't excuse what you did." Skirting her, he descended the steps to the deck and made his way around to the front of the house.

Jordan sank against the lounge chair near her, clasping its back to keep upright. Zachary's intenseness had sucked the energy from her, and she would need all she had to speak with Nicholas before he went to bed.

She would love to postpone this conversation. Forever. But she couldn't.

Lord, I know I was wrong. Please help me to fix this with Nicholas. I need You more than ever.

Shoving away from the chair, she headed for the door, then up the stairs toward her son's bedroom. She and Nicholas had always been close. This wouldn't change that. She hoped.

She rapped on his door, then entered, expecting him to be at his computer since he hadn't been in the bathroom. Instead the chair was empty. When she scanned the room, she discovered him already under the covers, his head barely peeking out. He always prolonged going to sleep, hating to miss anything.

"Nicholas."

Nothing. Not a word. Not a movement, as though he had fallen asleep in that short amount of time. She knew better.

"Nicholas, we need to talk."

"I don't want to talk to you."

Chapter Six

Nicholas's words hurt, a pang piercing through Jordan's heart. As much as she wanted to leave and never have this conversation with her son, she crossed the room to his bed and sat. "Hon, I know you're angry at me, and I can't blame you."

His back to her, he hunched his shoulders, pulling the blanket up around his neck even more. "Why didn't you tell me?"

"I really don't have a good defense for that. All I can tell you is what I was feeling when I was young. I was scared, alone and determined that I could raise you by myself. After trying to call Zachary, I decided I couldn't force him to be involved in our lives if he didn't want to. I figured I could be enough for you."

Nicholas twisted around, his eyes red from crying.

The pain in those eyes amplified her own. With her hand trembling, she placed it on his blanket-clad leg. "Your father had joined the army and was posted overseas. I didn't know where. Then you came more than a month early. It was all I could do to handle that. I was wrong and I'm so sorry about that. I should have told him. I should have tried harder to track him down somehow. I should have told you, but I honestly didn't think Zachary wanted anything to do with me." *Which is still true. But he did want to be involved with Nicholas. I can't deny him that.*

Her son's forehead scrunched. "I don't know what to think anymore."

"I can understand that. Can you forgive me?"

He turned away. "I'm tired."

What a mess she'd made of everything because of pride. Zachary was furious with her, and worse, her son was disappointed in her. She'd seen it in his eyes. That look tore her heart in two with guilt.

Lord, what do I do?

But no ready answer came to mind. She sat for another minute staring at her child's rigid body beneath the blanket. All she wanted to do was gather him into her arms and hold on to him as she had when he was a little boy. Instead, she settled for leaning over and kissing his cheek.

He shrank away and pulled the blanket totally over his head.

With a deep sigh, she shoved to her feet and trudged toward the hallway. Coming back to her hometown was supposed to be a good move for her and Nicholas. But now her life was in more of a mess than ever before.

The next afternoon before Jordan went to pick up Nicholas from school and go to Zachary's ranch, she strolled down the street to her sister's house and rang the bell.

"I wondered if you would stop by today," Rachel said as she stepped to the side to let Jordan inside.

"Who called you? Mom?"

"This morning I got a call from Granny, then an hour later one from Mom."

Jordan plopped down on her sister's pristine white couch

in her formal living room off the foyer. How she managed to keep her home so clean with three kids was a marvel to Jordan. "Where are the twins?"

"At Mother's Day Out at the church. I have to pick them up in half an hour." She sat across from Jordan in a wing chair.

"So I'm assuming you know all the gory details?"

"Yep. What Granny left out, Mom was able to fill me in on. Your usual talkative son didn't say a word to you this morning before school."

Jordan shook her head. "What do I do? You've had more experience than me. I'm desperate."

"I'm not so sure I'm the one you should come to. I'm having problems with Taylor, and I don't see an end in sight. She's thirteen, and we're butting heads."

"What if Nicholas wants to go live with Zachary?" There. She'd said her greatest fear.

"You're going to have to share your son now."

Jordan's fingernails gouged her palms. "If you hadn't sent me to the ranch..." She couldn't finish the sentence. A lump jammed her throat.

"Zachary should be in Nicholas's life."

Jordan stared at her feet. "I know. I should have listened to you."

"Yeah, but then I've been telling you that all your life."

"You never regretted telling Taylor she was adopted?"

"No."

"Does she ask about her biological parents?"

"No, she knows that her dad and I really wanted her. And Nicholas knows how much you love him and wanted him. He'll come around when the newness wears off. Be patient."

"Patient? I'm not very good at that."

Rachel chuckled. "Boy, do I know. That's one of the reasons I sent you to the ranch. It would have only been a matter of time before you and Zachary ran into each other. This way it's over with, and you won't continue to run away from what you should have done eleven years ago."

"A warning would have been good."

"And you wouldn't have gone. I'm not stupid."

Rachel was her big sister but had always been a friend and confidant. The only thing they had ever really argued about was Zachary. "You know Zachary didn't purposefully ignore my calls back then."

"I figured as much. He's a good man. A tad stubborn but then you can be, too."

Jordan pushed to her feet. "I can tell I'm gonna get no sympathy from you."

"When you need it, I'll be here, little sis."

"I'd better go. If I'm late to pick up Nicholas, I'll really get the cold shoulder."

Rachel walked her to the door. "Give it time and pray about it. Nicholas will come around. You two have been through a lot, and he knows you'll always be there for him."

Fifteen minutes later Jordan picked up Nicholas at Key Elementary then headed toward the ranch. Her stomach roiled from the silence in the car. Her damp palms slipped on the steering wheel.

Halfway to their destination, she asked, "How was the last day at school?"

"'Kay."

"Any trouble?"

A grunt was the only answer to that question.

"After we go to the ranch, I thought we would stop and have dinner at The Green Shack. I know how much you've enjoyed it the couple of times we've gone."

Not a peep out of the child who often talked nonstop, especially when he was excited.

"Are you worried about today?"

He shook his head. She would have missed his answer if she hadn't glanced at him.

When the ranch entrance came into view, she wiped her hands one by one on her jeans, then gripped the steering wheel tighter. Sweat popped out on her forehead and upper lip. Maybe Nicholas wasn't worried, but she was. The only good thing about the day was that Zachary's mother wouldn't be there. If she'd only given him Jordan's message, she wouldn't be in this pickle. Then she remembered the first time she'd talked with Becca, who had promised to pass the message on to her mother. She'd only been there visiting. Had Becca done as she promised or had she kept it to herself?

Not sure where to go—the blue house, barn or Zachary's place, Jordan drove past his sister's and the barn. She stopped outside Zachary's white home. The second she parked, Nicholas leaped from the car at the same time the front door swung open. Zachary came out onto the porch, smiling at his son as he raced toward the steps. Nicholas threw his arms around his father's waist.

The sight of their embrace slammed into her chest. This was how it could have been if they'd stayed together. Only, she'd be part of that hug, as well. The scene before her faded away as if she were in someone else's world. Slowly she climbed from her Camaro and strode toward the house, nearly stumbling when Becca came outside. Right behind the woman was Ashley and two younger boys. Lastly Becca's husband appeared, a broad grin on his face as he shook her son's hand.

She'd hoped Zachary would ease her son into his family but most of them were here now. The only thing missing were his parents. Already overwhelmed, she checked behind Becca's husband to make sure no one else was there.

Almost to the bottom stair, Zachary disengaged himself from his family. "You all go on inside. It's a scorcher out here."

Somehow she ended up at the bottom of the steps. She put her foot on the first stair.

Zachary stood before her. "If you don't want to stay, I can bring Nicholas home later this evening."

Meeting his gaze that had softened for a few seconds, she planted her feet on the next step. "That's okay. I don't mind staying." She forced a smile that quivered and fell.

"Suit yourself." He opened the screen door and headed inside.

Leaving Jordan standing on his porch by herself. She wasn't welcome at this little family party, but she didn't care. She was crashing it anyway. She wouldn't lose her son to the Rutgerses.

When she entered the living room, crammed with Zachary's family, she found Nicholas on the couch between Becca and Zachary. The only place for her to sit was a lounger set a little ways from the others—as though she were purposefully being excluded. She eased into the recliner, its worn comfortableness luring her into relaxation after getting almost no sleep the night before.

She looked around her, caught sight of a magazine about ranching, opened on the table near her elbow. When she drew in a deep breath, she thought she could smell Zachary's earthy scent embedded in the brown leather of the chair. The sense of him surrounding her zapped her. Her heart pounded against her chest. She was tied to Zachary now whether she wanted to be or not. She swiped her hand across the beads of perspiration on her upper lip. All the good times they'd spent together as teenagers paraded across her mind, taunting her with what she'd missed out on.

Becca rose from the couch and approached Jordan. "Would you help me get some drinks in the kitchen."

Jordan peered at her son, laughing at something Mike, Zachary's nine-year-old nephew, said. She nodded and rose, trailing behind the woman toward the kitchen. At the entrance into the room she glanced toward Nicholas. Zachary's pinpoint gaze snared hers and held it for a long moment. The sense of trespassing bathed her in a cold film.

"Which would Nicholas like—apple juice or lemonade?"

Becca's question dragged Jordan from the connection with Zachary. "He loves apple juice."

"So does Ashley but Mike and Cal like lemonade. That's why Zachary keeps both here. My children visit him a lot. This is a second home to them." Becca withdrew glasses from the cabinet. "What about you? Which would you like?"

"Neither."

Becca surveyed the contents of her brother's refrigerator. "There's tea in here, too. I have to admit little else, though."

"I'm not thirsty." Jordan stood in the middle of the kitchen. When Becca retrieved a small tray from a drawer, Jordan wondered why she was there.

"Can you fill those with ice?" Becca gestured toward the tumblers on the counter.

"Sure." Jordan didn't know Zachary's sister very well. When they had been dating, Becca had already been married a year and lived in Oklahoma City. That was why Jordan had been surprised that Becca had answered the phone when she'd called right after she'd found out she was pregnant.

"I thought you could use a breather."

"What do you mean?"

Becca lifted her shoulders in a shrug. "I figure this isn't easy for you."

Zachary's sister's words took Jordan by surprise. "You aren't mad at me?"

The woman paused and studied Jordan for a long moment. "No, not really. I should have asked you some questions when you called all those years ago. I could hear how upset you were. I should have made sure my mother gave Zachary the message."

Becca hadn't kept her call from Zachary. Somehow that comforted Jordan. "Why didn't she?" It might have changed everything.

"When I talked with her last night, she kept telling me she thought she was protecting Zachary from further hurt." Becca gave her a thin smile. "That's Mom for you. She-bear extraordinaire."

But Zachary's mother didn't have the right not to give her son the message. "Your brother doesn't care that I tried calling him."

"He's upset he didn't know about Nicholas until now. He'll get over it."

"I'm not so sure."

"Give him time. All of a sudden he's a father. It's a lot to take in. And you know men. They don't like to deal with emotions. They don't take them out and examine them to death like we do."

Jordan's tension eased. She relaxed against the counter. "He wasn't very good at telling me his feelings when we were teenagers."

"That hasn't changed in eleven years."

That was the crux of the problem. Even if Zachary could get past his anger at her, they had changed quite a bit from when they were two teenagers in love. They were really strangers who shared a son. She suddenly realized she wanted to get to know the man who was her child's father. Maybe there was hope for them.

"Thanks for letting me know not everyone in his family is mad at me."

Becca finished pouring the drinks and put the pitchers back in the near-empty refrigerator. "Nicholas is part of our family now, and you're part of his. I want this to work for everyone. Forgiveness is the only way to go. The Lord has it right. If we don't forgive, all we do is live in the past. I'm a present kind of gal." After handing Jordan two glasses of apple juice, Becca lifted the tray of lemonades. "Those are for Ashley and Nicholas."

Back in the living room, Jordan gave her son and the young girl their drinks, then took her chair again. This time calmness—a remnant from earlier in the kitchen—cloaked her. Forgiveness. Would Zachary ever be able to do that? Would she, for that matter? She still held scraps of anger toward him, especially when she thought about the pain of his rejection—being scared and alone, waiting for his calls that never came. But then she remembered he'd been clueless about her calls and what little anger was left melted away. She couldn't blame him for something he didn't know.

"We're gonna grill hamburgers for dinner up at our house. I hope you brought a big appetite, Nicholas." Becca set her glass on a coaster on the coffee table.

"I don't eat meat."

"You don't?" Zachary glanced from his son to Jordan. "Are you a vegetarian, too?"

"No, I'm not a purist like Nicholas. I occasionally eat meat."

"Mom tries to support my beliefs as much as possible."

"Okay—" Zachary ran his hand through his hair "—I'm sure we can find something for you to eat."

"I've got peanut butter," Becca piped in.

"I like that."

Mike studied his cousin. "Do you eat pizza?"

"Sure, cheese and a vegetable one."

"Yuck! I hate vegetables." Six-year-old Cal squirmed on the floor by his dad's feet.

"Mom makes a great one." Nicholas peered toward her. "She's the best cook."

Jordan released a slow breath. He might be upset with her right now, but his comments gave her hope she would be able to make it right with him soon. She needed to give her son time to bond with Zachary and his family. She owed Zachary that much.

Rising, she said, "I'll leave you all to enjoy your dinner. Zachary, what time should I come back to pick up Nicholas?"

"I'll bring him home."

"Fine." Overwhelmed by the past week, Jordan hurried from the house, fighting tears just below the surface. At her car she hesitated, staring at Zachary's home. For her son's sake, she and Zachary needed to get along. Could they come to an understanding?

My life is a mess, and I only have myself to blame.

Zachary pulled to a stop in front of Jordan's place and glanced at his son in the front seat of his truck. "If your mom says okay, grab your pj's and some clothes for tomorrow. We'll do some riding before some kids come for a lesson."

"Super."

He started to say, "Let me talk with your mother first," when Nicholas hopped down from the cab and raced toward the house.

As Zachary ambled toward the porch, his son announced his plans to Jordan, then scurried away—presumably up the stairs to get his stuff to stay overnight with him. When he mounted the steps, she came out onto the porch.

The light from the house illuminated her concern. Her beauty, which had plagued his dreams many nights, touched his core, tempting him to forget the last eleven years. "I get it that you want to make up for lost time, but you don't have to cram it all into the first few days. Nicholas has a habit of tiring himself out, then he gets sick."

He came to a halt a couple of feet from her, close enough to get a whiff of her vanilla scent. At least that hadn't changed in eleven years even if just about everything else had. Her fragrance stirred memories best left locked away. Zachary backed away to give himself some space. But he couldn't forget the times he'd held her close enveloped in the vanilla-laced fragrance. "I'll make sure he doesn't overdo it. He asked if he could. He wants to see what I do. I didn't see any reason to say no."

"How about the fact that I was starting his homeschooling tomorrow?"

"One of the nice things about teaching your child at home is that your schedule is flexible. You decide the when and where."

"I know we have to work out some kind of arrangement, but please run things by me before you say anything to Nicholas. He's been through a lot in his short life." Her voice quivered.

He could never resist the urge in the past to soothe away her concerns. This was no different. "Are you talking about the surgery to repair his heart defect?"

She nodded. "What did he tell you?"

"That his doctor says he's fine now. Fixed."

"That doesn't mean he shouldn't be careful."

"He'll be safe. I just found my son. I'm not gonna let anything happen to him, but I have a lot of catching up to do." He wanted this to work out for Nicholas's sake.

Tears misted Jordan's eyes. "I want this to work out for Nicholas. In order for that to happen, we need to be a team. Can you put aside your anger at me so we can work together for—our son?"

Chapter Seven

Jordan's unshed tears nearly undid Zachary. His gut tightened as though preparing to be hit. "You want the honest truth?"

"Always."

"I don't know. Yesterday morning I knew nothing about having a son. Then you appear and tell me Nicholas is my child. I'm still trying to digest what you told me. I need time."

"Fair enough." Jordan closed her eyes for a few seconds, a tear leaking out and running down her cheek.

The sight of it jolted him back to another time when they had fought and parted—her going to Savannah while he stayed in Tallgrass licking his wounds. Where would they be now if they had never fought that day or his mother had told him about Jordan's calls?

"Nicholas's welfare is the most important thing to me, so I want this to work. If we fight all the time and use him as a pawn in some game, he'll be the one who ends up hurt the most."

"Agreed. Let's start over. I'm Zachary Rutgers. I raise quarter horses and have a small herd of buffalo on my ranch." He held out his hand, shoving his anger away. He'd loved her at one time—knew she had a good heart. Working as a team—as Nicholas's parents—was what was best for their son.

She fit hers in his grasp and shook it. "I'm Jordan Masterson. I have a graphic design business and as of today I'm homeschooling my child and terrified I'm going to mess it up."

The warm feel of her fingers seared his palm. It took every ounce of willpower not to drop her hand, not to react to her touch, the softness of her skin against his work-toughened flesh. "I'll try to help with the homeschooling. I've picked up some things from Becca. And I know my sister would help you." Releasing her, he inhaled deeply. He could do this—be on friendly terms with Jordan—but he would make sure he guarded his heart. He wouldn't let her hurt him again.

"It'll be all I can do to stay one step ahead of him, especially in math."

"Check with Ian Ferguson about his math group. I know Ian and Alexa are planning to leave after the New Year, but until then it could be a solution to Nicholas's math needs."

"I'll do that. Nancy Baker said something about that when I met with her last week."

The door opened behind Jordan, and Nicholas exited. "I've got everything."

"Let's go, partner."

Jordan stopped their son and hugged him. "I love you, Nicholas. I know you'll behave." She kissed his cheek.

"Ah, Mom." He tugged away and hurried down the stairs toward Zachary's truck.

The crestfallen look on Jordan's face prodded Zachary to move closer and touch her arm. "Just exerting his independence."

"I wish he'd wait a few years. I'm not ready for him to grow up."

At least she'd had the first ten years with Nicholas. Her words drove home the fact he'd lost out on so much of his only child's life. He stepped back from Jordan, stomping down the rising anger. A team—him and Jordan. He would make it work somehow. For their son.

"What do you want for breakfast?" Zachary looked in his refrigerator and saw the few food provisions he had. He should have gone grocery shopping, but he hadn't originally thought that Nicholas would spend the night. "I've got some milk. We could have cereal." He took the carton, opened it and smelled. The rancid aroma of sour milk accosted his nostrils. "On second thought, maybe we could go out for breakfast." He glanced toward his son standing by the kitchen sink.

"That's okay." Nicholas rubbed the sleep from his eyes. "I'll go get dressed."

"Thanks, partner." When his son left the kitchen, Zachary massaged his temples. What else was he forgetting? He wasn't starting out very good as a father. *Note to self: get food in the house. See what Nicholas likes. Find out everything I can from Jordan about him.*

When he heard a knock at the front door, he made his way toward it. Jordan stood on his porch with a sack full of food in her arms. The beat of his heart sped as if he was settling on the back of the bull in the chute—seconds before the gate opened. He moved to the side and allowed her into his house, actually pleased at her appearance.

"I saw your empty refrigerator yesterday and figured you might not have much for breakfast, so here I am. I can make both of you buttermilk pancakes. Okay?" She turned in the foyer and waited for his answer.

She was trying to make the best of their situation. He needed to meet her halfway. "I haven't had pancakes in a long time."

"And you used to love them."

"Still do."

"So does Nicholas." She started for the kitchen.

Zachary followed her and watched from the doorway while she made herself at home, taking the food out of the sack and putting some of it away while setting the rest on the counter to use. The sight of her in his kitchen reconstructed some of his past dreams when he'd thought they would marry. He couldn't emotionally afford those dreams, and yet she fit well into his kitchen.

"Blackberries are in right now. I use them as a topping. Remember that time we went blackberry picking? That snake that slithered among the bushes?" She opened a cabinet and withdrew a mixing bowl, then threw a glance over her shoulder.

"You couldn't move fast enough."

"Right into your arms. All I could think about was getting my feet off the ground," she said with a laugh. "That seems to be my reaction when I see a snake."

The sound of her merriment drew him forward. Crossing the kitchen, he kept his gaze on her. All of a sudden he was whisked back to when he was eighteen, in love with her, spending a morning picking blackberries because she asked him sweetly to help her. Her grandmother was going to make her blackberry jam and needed some fresh ones. He'd been on top of the world, in spite of the snake that had quickly slid away, probably because of Jordan's loud scream.

"I never did get a jar of the jam." He stopped a few feet from her, their looks still entangled together.

"Neither did I." She blinked and averted her head.

"Yeah, you left for art school three weeks later."

The air thickened with charged emotions. Recalling that time brought bittersweet memories to the foreground. Zachary clamped down on his jaw to keep the words from boiling to the surface. Words of recrimination. If only the past had been different, they would be a couple now. If only... He had to stop feeling this way. He needed to live in the present.

"Mom, what are you doing here?"

Jordan whirled around, a grin on her face. "Rescuing your dad with breakfast."

Your dad. Zachary liked the sound of that.

Nicholas checked out the ingredients on the counter. "Buttermilk pancakes?"

She nodded.

His son pumped his arm in the air. "Wait till you eat them, Dad."

Dad! That was the first time Nicholas had said it. The best sound in the world. It filled him with joy. "Can I do anything to help?"

She waved her hand. "No, you two go somewhere and get to know each other. I'll call you when I've got it fixed."

He studied Jordan for a moment. What was this Jordan like? She wasn't a teenager anymore. He suddenly wanted to know the woman standing before him. Maybe then they could be the team Nicholas needed. "We'll be out on the porch."

"Great. It'll be about fifteen minutes."

Outside Nicholas sat on the top stair next to Zachary. His son set his forearms on his thighs just like him, clasping his hands loosely.

"Did you ask Mom to come?"

"No, but I guess yesterday she saw how pitiful my food supply is."

"She's perceptive like that."

"Yeah, and better organized than I am."

"I find if you're organized it saves a lot of useless time looking for things you've misplaced."

Zachary chuckled. "You're one hundred percent right. You two will have to rub off on me."

"How did you and Mom meet?"

The question flooded him with memories—all good ones. "I was on the football team in high school. A fullback. It was the first game, and not far from where I was sitting on the bench waiting for the offense to get their turn to play, I spied your mom cheering. She was the new one on the squad. I caught her gaze. As we were staring at each other, she missed her move and the girl next to her ran into her. She blushed a nice shade of red. Matched her uniform. Of course, after the game I had to apologize."

"So you two started dating?"

The journey into the past prodded good memories into his mind. But she wasn't the same. He wasn't the same, either. Zachary kneaded the cords of his neck. Too tight— tight as the cinch on a saddle. "Well, not exactly. It took me a few weeks to wear her down. She was embarrassed in front of the student body. A piece of advice for the future. Not the best way to meet a gal."

"You played football. I don't know anything about the game. Isn't it just a bunch of guys trying to hurt each other?"

"I can see where you might think that. When I played, I learned teamwork."

Nicholas's gaze skimmed down his length. "I'm too small to play football."

"The game isn't for everyone. There are other sports if you want to do something like that. Soccer doesn't depend on size. Have you thought of that?"

His son shook his head. "I'm not very coordinated."

"I could work with you if you want to practice handling a ball." Zachary placed his hand on his son's shoulder. "But you don't have to. It's your call. Just know I'll help you any way you want."

Nicholas flashed him a huge grin.

In that second a bond formed between him and his son. Emotions he'd guarded welled up into his throat, sealing words inside—words he wasn't good at saying.

"Breakfast is served." Jordan stood at the screen door.

Zachary swallowed several times and breathed in the coffee-laced air. "You fixed coffee, too?" The wobble in his voice hung suspended for a few seconds between them.

"Sure. I know how you like it. I pitched yours." She winced. "I'm gonna have to teach you how to brew a good cup."

She'd always been a good cook. "I may take you up on that." Zachary rose, brushing his hand down his jeans.

Nicholas did the same thing, dust flying everywhere. Zachary needed to sweep his steps. His son began coughing. Jordan started toward him but stopped halfway there and remained still.

"Did you bring apple juice?" Nicholas asked after sucking in several deep breaths.

"Your dad still had some left from yesterday. I poured you a glass. It's on the table."

Nicholas hurried into the house while Zachary said, "Housekeeping has never been my forte."

"To tell you the truth it isn't mine, either. Give me something to cook and I'm happy. Give me a dust rag and I find a way to get out of it."

Zachary swiped a hand across his forehead. "Whew, I'm relieved. It's bad enough I don't cook well, but I hated to fall short in every area."

Jordan paused in the foyer. "This isn't a competition."

"I know but I've spent a good part of my life competing—first on the football field and then in the rodeo ring."

"What did you two talk about?"

He grinned and winked at her. "How you and I met."

A faint blush tinted her cheeks, again reminding him of their first encounter. "Did you mention I fell flat on my bottom in front of a stadium full of people?"

"Sort of, but I took full blame for the accident."

"Oh, that is so reassuring." Jordan marched past him.

He admired how cute she was when she blushed. Putting the brakes on the directions his thoughts were going, he shook his head then proceeded into the kitchen a few steps behind her. Friends—that was all they could be now.

"Where have you guys been? I'm starving."

"Did you wash your hands?" Jordan asked as she sat across from her son.

Zachary diverted his path to the sink and made sure he did exactly what Jordan had asked Nicholas. He had to set a good example for his son.

"Yes, I did. I know how important good hygiene is. So many of our germs are spread by hand contact. That's why they stress washing so much during flu season."

Zachary listened to his son launch into the health risk when people didn't follow that simple rule, even quoting a medical source. That was when he knew he was in over his head and drowning.

Two days later on Saturday afternoon Jordan turned into the ranch to pick up her son after he'd spent another night at Zachary's. When Nicholas had returned home after the first time, all he could talk about was how neat it was to own a ranch. He had her take him to the library and he got every book he could find on the subject of horses. As she pulled up next to Zachary's Ford F-150 truck near the barn, she wondered how the joint grocery store trip went last evening. He had wanted Nicholas to go with him so he got all their son's favorite food.

As Jana strolled with Alexa toward an SUV, Jordan climbed from her Camaro and waved. With quick steps she covered the area between them. "I'm glad I caught you before you left."

Alexa grinned. "I hear you're taking the plunge and homeschooling Nicholas."

"Yeah, and I'm suddenly freaking out. What if I don't do a good job? What was I thinking that I could teach my child? I haven't had any training at all. This week was my first, and I felt so out of my comfort zone."

"You aren't alone. Ian told me he felt the same way when he first started. Probably still does."

"But he has you. You're almost through with your education degree."

Alexa leaned close as Jana climbed into the front seat of the SUV. "I have my doubts at least once a week. It's a big decision to become solely responsible for a child's education. The fact you don't take it lightly means you'll do fine."

"I was hoping to catch you today. I want to sign Nicholas up for Ian's new class."

"Great. I'll tell him. It starts next week on Wednesday at one."

Releasing a sigh, Jordan relaxed. "At least that's one worry taken care of. But then I'll have to relearn algebra all over again in order to help him. I bought a book this morning. It's been years since I had any."

"If you get stuck, I'm sure Ian will help you." Alexa opened her door and settled behind the steering wheel. "You could even take the class with Nicholas."

"Thanks. I'll think about that." Jordan headed forward. That was one problem she could mark off her long list. She'd started reading the curriculum she'd borrowed from Nancy. If it fit Nicholas, she would purchase the books and use them as a framework to teach him. Having a structure at least made her feel better—like a pilot having a flight plan.

Inside the barn she paused at the entrance to scan the area for her son. Out the back double doors she glimpsed him with Zachary. As she ambled toward them, Zachary demonstrated how to rope a steer by using a bale of hay with a cow head made of plastic stuck in one end.

When Nicholas took his rope and swung it over his head from right to left, Zachary said, "Keep swinging, but bring it out in front of you and remember when you release it to point your finger toward the steer."

Nicholas let go and the loop landed on the hay. "I don't think I can do this."

"Yes, you can. It just takes practice." Zachary released his rope, and it sailed over the horn and around the fake steer's head.

"And why would you want to do it?" Jordan asked as she came up to the pair.

Eyes round, Nicholas stared at Zachary. "It's part of being a cowboy."

"A cowboy? Since when did you want to be one?" The last time she'd talked with her son, he'd wanted to be an engineer. Of course, that was before he'd found out Zachary was his father.

Her son straightened, his shoulders back. "I want to help Dad on the ranch. I've got to know these things."

The second Nicholas said *Dad* Zachary beamed, crinkling the corners of his eyes. "I was showing him how to throw a rope. He was asking me about some of the activities I've done in a rodeo."

"Rodeo! No, sir. You won't go near a rodeo."

"Why not? Once I learn to ride, I can do all kinds of things. I've seen some videos on the Internet. There's barrel racing, for one."

There were those words again. What was it about dangerous sports and men? The time Zachary had flown off his horse, racing, and crashed into the dirt flashed through her mind. For long seconds he hadn't moved, and it seemed as if her heart had stopped beating for that time. When he finally had stirred, he'd broken his arm. Jordan stuffed her hands into her jeans pockets to still their trembling. The image of Zachary injured blurred with a similar picture of her son, lying still, in pain. She couldn't separate the two in her mind. The insight stunned her. Did she still have deep feelings for Zachary?

He clasped Nicholas on the shoulder. "I think that's enough practice for today. Why don't you go say goodbye to Chief?"

Her son peered from Zachary to her then back. "Sure. I'll mosey on over to the paddock. Let me know when you two finish jawing."

Jordan's mouth fell open at the sound of Nicholas trying to imitate some cowboy from a B movie. "What have you done to my son?"

"Nothing. He wanted me to show him the ropes of being a rancher today. He rode with me to check some fences, helped me fix one section. We stacked hay bales. He learned to muck out a stall."

"Muck out a stall? Nicholas?" He rarely got down and dirty.

"Yep, little lady, you've got that right." Hooking his thumbs in his waistband, Zachary winked at her.

"I can't believe…" Her words spluttered to a halt like a runaway calf roped by a cowboy.

Nicholas was a scholar. He lived in books and loved to read and study. Yes, he should do some physical activity, but mucking a stall and stacking hay bales was hard work. Filthy work. "I agreed that my son could learn to ride a horse, but that was all. Nothing else beyond that and certainly nothing that might lead him to believe he could perform in a rodeo. Look what happened to you." She gestured toward Zachary's leg that had been broken while riding a bull, bred to buck and twist and trample anyone in its way. At least that was what Nicholas had told her.

"I zigged when I should have zagged." Although he shrugged, the set of his shoulders sank back into a tensed stance. "It happens sometimes to a bull rider. I knew the risk when I took up the profession." If he'd known what he could have lost—his ability to have children—would he have still risked riding a bull? He'd loved the thrill. For eight seconds on the back of a bull, he'd come alive. He hadn't felt that way—like anything was possible—since he and Jordan had dated. Now he knew anything was possible only through the Lord.

"My son isn't gonna do anything remotely like that. Is that what you want for Nicholas?"

He pressed his lips together for a few seconds, causing a quiver in his facial muscle. "I don't know my son well enough to start dreaming his future. I do know I will not dictate what he does but guide him."

She stepped back. "Ha! This from a man who has been a father for half a week. Walk in my shoes for a few years or for that matter months then tell me you won't worry about his choices and try and change the ones that aren't good."

"Hey, guys, you're shouting," Nicholas yelled from the fence.

She moved within inches of Zachary and lowered her voice. "He's fragile. He gets sick easily and doesn't need to do a lot of physical activity. Just a little."

"Why? He was fine today. I thought his heart defect was fixed." Was there something he didn't know? He was discovering so much about Nicholas—and Jordan. What had made her so afraid of life? He wanted to know. He wanted to get reacquainted with Jordan. Stunned by the thought, he curled his hands into fists and jammed them into his pockets.

"It is, but we still go to the cardiologist for checkups. He has one with his new doctor in a week in Tulsa."

Zachary folded his arms over his chest. "I'm going with you. Let's talk to his doctor about how much activity Nicholas can do and what kind. Let him decide." Nicholas was his one chance at being a father. He had to know his son would be okay. He narrowed his look and dared her to take the challenge.

"Okay. A deal. If the doctor says he can do more, I'll consider it."

The second she agreed, he thought of being in a car for two hours with Jordan. He didn't like the emotions Jordan stirred alive in him. He didn't want to remember the past, to care for her. That gave her the power to hurt him all over again. "No, Nicholas will then have the choice. He's my son, too." His gaze strayed to their child. "I'm warning you now that Nicholas wants to ride in the barrel race during the HHH Junior Rodeo competition next month. He's asked me to help him. There are two events set. One for beginners and another for advanced riders. He'll be able to do the beginner one. He's a natural when it comes to riding."

"Why can't he run in some other race like the fifty-yard dash?"

"Because he told me he doesn't run fast and isn't strong. I think he believes being on a horse makes him more equal physically to the other kids. It requires a certain amount of skill, which he thinks he can learn."

"He probably can if he sets his mind to it."

"Speaking of mind, just how smart is Nicholas?"

"When he was tested, his IQ was one hundred sixty-two."

Zachary whistled. "I'm gonna have to hustle to keep up with him."

"Welcome to my world. There are words he'll throw out when telling me about something he's read that I've got to go and look up their definition."

Her chuckles sprinkled the air with her amusement. The sound reminded Zachary of a time when they had been carefree teens dating, falling in love. He couldn't shake the question: what could have happened between them if he'd received her messages?

But he hadn't. She was a good mother—a bit overprotective but Nicholas was a fine young man. Jordan had always wanted three or four children, and she should have them. He couldn't give her what she always talked about. He had to accept that fact and try to keep his distance.

Chapter Eight

"Hi, Granny. What are you doing out here?" That evening Nicholas plopped down next to his great-grandmother on the porch swing.

"Enjoying the beautiful evening while waiting for my friend. How did you enjoy your day with your dad?"

"I'm learning everything I can about ranching. Did you know that Dad has a pregnant mare? She should give birth any day. I hope I'm there when she does. I've seen videos, but I'd like to see it in real life. The more I'm around the animals the more I'm thinking of being a vet instead of an engineer."

"That's a wonderful profession. So you don't have dreams of going on the rodeo circuit like your dad?"

Nicholas shook his head. "Me? I found a clip online of when my dad got hurt at the National Finals." A shudder rattled down him as if he was in his dad's truck bumping over rough terrain.

"Did your mom see it?"

"No. She would freak out. It made me think twice about learning to ride. But then he was on a bull. A horse is different." Nicholas remembered the feel of power beneath him, the sense of freedom when he'd ridden. "I like how I feel when I'm riding."

Granny patted his leg. "Well, a word of advice, don't let your mom see that clip. She *will* freak out. She used to when Zachary was in a rodeo when they were in high school. She hasn't totally learned that the Lord is in control. She still tries to control everything."

"I know." Nicholas leaned against the side of the swing, fitting his chin in his palm. "Dad told me how he met Mom today. When he talked about it, he smiled. There was a look on his face that makes me think he still likes Mom even though they fight."

"They're fighting?" One of Granny's penciled-in eyebrows rose.

"I heard them today, fighting over me. I don't want to be the reason they're arguing."

"Then we need to do something about that."

"What?"

"How about we give them something else to think about? It's time those two got together for good. They're meant to be a couple. They just don't know it."

Nicholas angled toward Granny. "Fix them up? I like it. What can we do?"

"Well—" she rubbed her chin "—let me think a second. Maybe you could have them both take you somewhere."

"Dad's going with us to Tulsa this week to see my cardiologist."

"Good. That's a start." Granny snapped her fingers. "I've got it. Homecoming at Tallgrass High School is in two weeks. Get your dad and mom to take you to the game. You know your dad played football?"

"He told me. I guess I could. I've never understood the lure of the game, but maybe if I went with Dad, I could see what the big deal is."

"Yeah, a lot of folks around here live for the games on Friday nights."

"We'll be in the middle of a lot of people in the stands. How's that going to help?"

"Time spent together is good. They need to get to know each other again. A lot has happened in eleven years." A brilliant smile lit his great-grandmother's face, the dark twinkle illuminating her mischief. "And I'll get them to take Mr. Bateman and me to the Alumni Homecoming Dance the following night."

"You're going to a dance?"

Straightening, she peered down her nose at Nicholas, both eyebrows lifting. "I'll have you know I'm eighty years young and can still dance."

"I think this can work. I'll say something on the trip to Tulsa." Nicholas hugged Granny, kissing her cheek. "You're the best."

Two patches of red colored her face. She looked beyond Nicholas. The impish gleam metamorphosed into a sparkle of delight. "My date is here. Help me up."

As Nicholas assisted his great-grandmother to her feet, a thin, balding man with a matching glimmer in his brown eyes ascended the steps to the porch. "Do you want me to get your walker?"

"I've hidden that thing. I'm perfectly fine getting around on my own. And don't you forget it, young man."

"I won't, Granny."

After finishing her meal, Jordan sat back in her chair at the Osage Restaurant within Gilcrease Museum and stared out the floor-to-ceiling window that afforded a panoramic view of the surrounding hills. Across from her Zachary savored his last few bites. He glanced up and found her staring at him. She quickly returned her attention to the beautiful scenery outside. She enjoyed watching Zachary. Always had.

Nicholas stuffed the last of his cheese pizza into his mouth then finished off his milk. "May we stop by the museum gift shop before we leave? I want to see if they have any books about the tribes that settled in this area. I haven't read much on them yet, but don't you think that should be something I study, Mom? Oklahoma is unique. Over half the state was Indian Territory until the early twentieth century."

"I remember once in elementary school we reenacted a land rush like they did to settle part of Oklahoma." Jordan sank back in her chair, relaxed despite Zachary being so close. The visit to the cardiologist had gone well. Nicholas was happy. Today for a short time at the doctor's she'd felt as though they were truly a family. She'd liked that feeling.

"Some people cheated and jumped the gun. They snuck onto the land ahead of time and staked their claim. Those folks were called Sooners, and that's where the name Sooner State came from." Zachary lifted his iced tea and took the last few swallows of it.

"Isn't the University of Oklahoma's football team called the Sooners? They have a good football tradition there."

Surprised by her son's comment, Jordan stared at him. "I didn't know you followed college football."

"I haven't, but Granny told me football is important to this area so I've been reading about it. I think I have most of the rules figured out, but I'd like to go to a game. Granny said something about Tallgrass High School where you two went is having its homecoming game next Friday night. Will you take me?" Nicholas swung his gaze from her to Zachary. "It would be fun to go together."

The last sentence thrown out so casually made Jordan

shift and study Zachary's suddenly unreadable expression. Going to a football game with Zachary would certainly bring back memories of how it had once been between them. Was that wise? "I don't—"

"Please, Mom, Dad."

"Sure, why not. I had planned to attend, and it would be easy for me to swing by and pick up you two."

"That's fine with me." There was no way she would be the one to say no, not with her son looking eagerly at her. But the idea of football and Nicholas didn't go together. She would go for no other reason than to make sure her son didn't decide he should play the game like his father had. Picturing kids twice Nicholas's body mass barreling into him sent a shudder through her. But she was concerned visiting their old high school haunts would make her dream of a future with Zachary. A risk she would have to take.

"I do have a question." Nicholas's forehead crinkled. "How come it's called football? From what I've found you use your foot more in a game like soccer than you do in football."

"You're right. And in other parts of the world soccer is called football."

"It makes more sense," Nicholas said in a serious tone.

"What would you call it?" Zachary took out his money to pay the check.

"Tackleball. It seems like that is the focus of the game."

Leave it for her son to question the name of a national sport. "I think you have something there."

"Ready to go to the museum shop?" Zachary rose.

Nicholas hopped up and hurried ahead of them out of the restaurant.

"I guess he's ready," Zachary said, the laugh lines at the sides of his eyes deepening.

"Dangle a book in front of him and he can move fast." Jordan paused outside the gift shop in the museum hall. "You aren't gonna encourage him to play football, are you?"

"No, in fact, we talked about it last week. I suggested if he wanted to play a sport soccer might be a better fit. But ultimately I want Nicholas to do what he wants. If his heart isn't in it, it's a waste of time."

"A parent has to sometimes say no to certain activities."

"True, but there's nothing wrong with soccer. Yes, he could get hurt, but he also could crossing a street." His gaze fastened onto hers, narrowed slightly. "But soccer isn't what you're really worried about. You think he'll want to participate in rodeo events like I did."

"Just because the doctor said exercise would be great for Nicholas doesn't mean he should do that." Zachary's triumphant expression at the cardiologist's office played across her mind. She drew herself up taller.

He cut the space between them. "Do you think I'd purposely put our child in danger?"

The low rumble of his voice rolled over her. "Well, no."

"A lot of events in a junior rodeo are safe. As safe as any other sport. You won't always be able to protect him. What parents do is prepare their children the best they can and then leave the rest in the Lord's hands. What are you really afraid of?"

Being on the outside looking in. Losing Nicholas to you. Losing control of my life. But she couldn't tell Zachary that. When she'd nearly lost her son, she'd clung to anything that she could control. She set up a routine for herself and

Nicholas, and it had worked until she'd moved back to Tallgrass. Now she was struggling to fit homeschooling into their lives. And to fit Zachary into their lives. "What any mother would be afraid of."

As she started for the gift shop, he stilled her movements with a hand on her arm. "I want what is best for our son, too."

She could barely concentrate on what Zachary was saying. His touch branded her his. She was going to get hurt.

"I'm just finding out how bright he is. But I also see his shortcomings. He isn't comfortable with his peers. He's even told me that. Thankfully he and Randy have hit it off, but then Randy is a smart kid, too, so they talk the same language. He has trouble doing things with his hands like tying a knot for his rope. He isn't in the best physical shape. He probably sits too much at a computer. He needs to be more active."

His words slammed her defenses in place. "He's not playing video games. He's researching. He uses the computer for just about everything because his handwriting is not legible." Needing to sever their physical connection, she pulled her arm from his grasp and backed away. This way she could think straight while around Zachary.

"I'm being realistic here. I'm not putting him down. Like everyone, he has strengths and weaknesses."

She knew that. And what Zachary said was true. Her son needed to work on his social skills as well as his fine motor ones. He needed to become more physical.

Zachary moved again into her personal space and glanced over her shoulder into the store before he returned his gaze to her. "I may not have the book smarts like Nicholas and you, but I can help our son. Let me help him become more active. Get more involved in life and the people around him."

For a moment she wanted to protest. She was doing a good job with her son. Then she remembered the doctor had suggested he do more physically, that he was perfectly healthy now. Finally she said, "I'm doing the best I can."

"And anyone who sees you two together sees the bond you all have. I'm continually amazed at how smart Nicholas is, and you've cultivated that. You're willing to give up your time to homeschool him because he isn't thriving in a public school. No one doubts the type of mother you are."

His praise lifted her shoulders, raised her chin a notch. He thought she was a good mother. That meant a lot—perhaps too much.

"But I want to be his father. I want to share equally in raising him. But you're still holding on so tight."

His words deflated her, lashing like a whip against a horse's flank. She blew a breath out. "You don't pull any punches, do you?"

"No, this is too important. I'll make you a promise. I won't let Nicholas do anything he isn't prepared to do. He's too important for me to do that."

"I'll try my best. Now I'd better go get Nicholas. It's gonna be late when we get back to Tallgrass." Needing some distance from him, Jordan quickly entered the store. Each day she was with Zachary more of her heart surrendered to him. And that scared her.

Zachary stayed in the hall, waiting while Nicholas paid for a book he wanted to buy. This was his one shot at being a father. He didn't want to screw it up.

Am I doing the right thing, Lord? How does a parent know if he is? He felt like the first time he rode a bull: ill prepared. In over his head, careening toward disaster.

"Look at the book I got, Dad. It's all about the tribes that settled this part of the Oklahoma."

His son's contagious smile warmed Zachary. He'd make mistakes—what parents didn't—but Nicholas would always know he loved him. "My great-grandmother was part of the Osage tribe."

"Really? Then that's the first one I'll research."

"C'mon. We need to get on the road. I have a pregnant mare to check on."

"Will you let me know when she's going to give birth?"

"Sure."

Nicholas turned toward his mother. "Then you can bring me out to the ranch. Maybe I can be there for it. It could be a biology lesson."

Jordan nabbed Zachary's look. "If it's okay with you."

"It could be in the middle of the night. I try to bring my pregnant mares into the barn and keep an eye on them when their time gets close. Usually there isn't a problem, but my stock is important to me. I like to be there if something goes wrong." He held the door open for Nicholas and Jordan at the exit to the museum.

"That's okay with me. I can sleep the next day." Nicholas clutched his book to his chest.

"How about you, Jordan?"

"Sure. I'll have you call my cell so it won't disturb Mom or Granny. I'll warn them about what's going on so they won't worry if we aren't there in the morning."

So much for his vow not to spend time with Jordan. First the football game next Friday and now the birth of a foal. He found it hard to separate his feelings for his son and Jordan. And worse, her appeal was as strong as it was when he was a teenager. He wasn't the best man for Jordan. He couldn't give her what she wanted or needed—the same as in the past. She'd fled Tallgrass because she'd wanted something different. What was stopping her from doing that again? Fear and doubts intruded into his thoughts. Although he couldn't keep his distance, that didn't mean his heart would be involved.

"So how has it been so far?" Rachel sat where Zachary had been before halftime of the homecoming game on Friday night.

"Lonely." Jordan sipped her soft drink, watching the band march off the field.

"You've got thousands of people around you."

"Yeah, but Zachary and Nicholas deserted me to go to the locker room during halftime."

"I guess it pays to be male and know the head coach."

"I forgot that Zachary was good friends with him in high school."

"Feeling left out?"

Jordan slid a glare at her older sister. "Well, no, but even when I was cheerleading I didn't particularly like the game. At least with them here, the time goes fast."

"Ah, who are you missing more, Nicholas or Zachary?"

Heat scored Jordan's face. She gave Rachel another glare, hoping the set of her features conveyed the topic was off-limits.

Her sister held up her hands, palms outward. "Hey, it was just a question. A valid one at that."

"Don't you have to get back to the concession stand or something?"

"I only had to man it for the first half. I can join you all and watch the game." Rachel tucked her purse down by her feet. "I'm not into football much, but my daughter, believe it or not, is and I had to bring her. She's off with her friends right now. You know how thirteen-year-olds are. They want nothing to do with their moms. I offered to work concession as an excuse to be near Taylor."

"Ha!" Jordan waggled a finger at her sister. "I'm not the only one who overprotects their child."

"I have good reason. Taylor tends to get into trouble all the time. When has Nicholas?"

"He forgot to shut the gate last week, and Tucker got out of the backyard."

"I wish that was the worst thing my daughter did."

Jordan studied her sister's worried expression, eyebrows drawn together. "Can I help?"

"Actually I'm thinking of looking into homeschooling if things don't turn around at school for Taylor. She had to serve detention yet again—four times so far this year. I don't know her anymore."

"Since I haven't been doing it long, I would suggest you talk with Dr. Baker or even Zachary's sister. They know a lot more than I do."

"I thought homeschooling was going okay for you."

"It is. I think. Never thought I would be sitting in on a math class again. But when Nicholas is taking algebra at Ian's house, I'm right there, too."

"Maybe once he learns it, he can help Taylor, who is struggling in math."

Jordan caught sight of Nicholas running out onto the field with the football team. Zachary trailed behind him, talking with the coach. Her son's grin could be seen all the way up in the bleachers where she sat near the top.

"Nicholas looks happy. Zachary has been good for him," Rachel said.

Yeah, he has. "I just wish things were better between us."

"You two been fighting? I thought you told me you were working as a team."

"Yeah, but there's still a barrier between us. I don't think he's ever going to forgive me for not telling him about Nicholas."

"Give him time."

"You know me. Impatient. I want to control everything." Jordan tried to laugh it off, but the sound came out choked. She wanted more from Zachary. She didn't want to be just friends. She nearly dropped her soda. The realization astounded her. The intensity that cinched her insides chilled her. If she wasn't careful, she would fall in love with Zachary all over again.

"I hear Granny and Doug are double-dating with you and Zachary tomorrow night."

"Have you ever felt manipulated by our grandmother?"

Rachel smiled. "All the time. She's a pro."

"She didn't say anything to me. She asked Zachary when he brought Nicholas back home a few days ago. Granny said something about Doug's car not working or some such excuse that she and her beau needed a ride to the Alumni Homecoming Dance. And how going to the dance with me and him would be perfect. I could have died from embarrassment."

"But Zachary is taking you? Have I misunderstood?"

"Only because Granny worked her wiles on him. He could never resist her."

"So you're not looking forward to tomorrow night?"

Jordan watched Nicholas and Zachary making their way toward her in the stands. "I've already had several friends from high school ask us if we're dating again. It'll be far worse at the dance."

"Which is worse? It's not an actual date, or that you're friends think you two are dating again?"

Thankfully Zachary and Nicholas arrived before Jordan

had to answer her sister's question. She hated to admit out loud it was because it wasn't an actual date—one that Zachary had thought to ask her on.

"Mom, did you see me with the team?" Her son held up a football. "They all signed it for me."

"That's wonderful," Jordan said as Nicholas sat on the other side of Rachel and Zachary folded his long length in the place next to Jordan.

Zachary bent close to her ear. "You don't have to worry about him wanting to sign up for football tomorrow. He told me he was having a good time, but there was no way he would stand in front of a guy larger than him and let him mow him down. Football is not a sensible game to our son."

His breath tickled her neck. She shivered. How was she going to make it through tomorrow night?

Later that night, Zachary laid his son on his bed in his room. Nicholas stirred, his eyes fluttering open for a few seconds then closing. Rolling onto his side, he hugged his pillow.

Zachary sat beside Nicholas and untied his tennis shoes. "He wants a pair of cowboy boots." With a glance toward Jordan behind him, he gauged her reaction to that statement. A flicker of something blinked in and out of her eyes. A composed expression fell into place. "I told him I would take him to buy them."

Her neutral facial features didn't change. "That makes sense if he's going to be at the ranch a lot. He already has the cowboy hat. He might as well have the boots."

When Jordan approached the bed, he could smell the vanilla scent she always wore. Memories rushed forward. He shook his head and rose. Inhaling cleansing breaths, he watched Jordan bend over, kiss Nicholas and then pull a blanket up to his shoulders. Tender caresses. Loving gestures. Remembered ones.

She turned on his night-light and switched off the overhead one. "He's gonna sleep soundly tonight. He's exhausted."

"Yeah. One minute he was talking in the backseat and the next he was conked out."

"That's our son. One hundred percent whatever he does." Jordan descended the stairs to the first floor. "He really enjoyed meeting the team."

Our son. They shared a child. The idea still amazed him. He'd given up hope of ever having a child. "And now you don't have to worry he's gonna play football anytime soon. Did you see him wince every time the quarterback got sacked?"

As she ambled toward the front door, she threw him a grateful smile, a shade of relief leaking into her eyes. "Yeah. I'd forgotten how much I hated seeing you play. I held my breath whenever you were tackled."

"That's part of the game."

She tsked. "Men and their sports."

"Women play sports, too."

"We're not generally out on the football field tackling each other."

"True." He stepped out onto the porch and swung around to face her. "It's nice to see some things haven't changed. You're still a softie."

"And proud of it."

The tilt of her lifted chin, the sparkle in her eyes brought back more memories. Ones he couldn't hold at bay. Her challenging him to a horse race she knew she would lose. She'd only been riding a few months, but he had most of his life. Or the time she'd played a practical joke on him that had backfired. She'd laughed at herself, drenched with water, her long blond curls limp about her face, her dark eyes dancing as she had backed away from the hose.

"Oh, that reminds me. Nicholas wants to bring Tucker to the ranch next time he goes. He thinks his dog will enjoy the space to run." She shifted from one foot to the other.

"Sure, we can try it. If Tucker gets along with the other animals, he'll be fine."

Jordan moved out onto the porch, the light from the foyer not quite reaching her face. "Are you all right about taking Granny and Doug to the dance?"

"Are you kidding? I can't wait to see your grandmother dancing."

"She told me once she was quite a ballroom dancer, but since she has trouble walking, I don't think she'll do much tomorrow evening."

"I have a feeling your grandmother can do just about anything she sets her mind to."

Her laughter echoed in the night. Its sound washed over him in more remembrances of shared amusement and lured him closer to her. He cupped her face still hidden in the shadows and wished the barriers between them were gone. He couldn't trust the feelings stirring deep in his heart.

"You do realize Granny manipulated us into taking her?"

Her question came out in a breathless rush that jolted his heartbeat into a faster tempo. "Yes, from the beginning. This isn't really a double date."

Beneath his palm she tensed. "Yeah, we're just—" there was a long pause "—friends."

Her words unsettled him. He wanted more and couldn't risk it. Nicholas was not enough of a reason to take their relationship any further than friendship. And there were barriers to anything more. "Just friends," he repeated as though he needed to emphasize it to himself rather than Jordan.

She began to pull back. His hand tightened. She stilled, the rapid rise and fall of her chest attesting to her charged emotions. Ones that mirrored his. He wanted to kiss her. To feel one more time her lips against his. For old times' sake.

Chapter Nine

The direction of Zachary's thoughts brought him up short. Falling back into that old pattern wouldn't be good for either one. They had their chance once, and it hadn't worked out. He had to remember that.

He backed away, his hand dropping to his side. "I'd better go." Another foot back. "I'll see Nicholas for his riding lesson. There's a place I wanted to show Nicholas and the others." His palms sweaty, he buried them into the depths of his front pockets. "You can come if you want. You might enjoy seeing the place."

"What is it?" Jordan moved into the stream of light from the foyer.

He still wanted to kiss her. His gaze fastened on her lips. "My secret."

She flinched when he said the word *secret*. That evasive flicker he'd seen a moment before blazed a second. Died. "I can't. Alexa is taking Nicholas for me."

"How about I bring him home when I come to pick you and Granny up tomorrow evening?" Disappointment edged his voice. He heard it and prayed she didn't. "He can help me get ready. I've got to find my suit."

"At least you don't have to go buy a dress. Rachel has decided to give me her expert advice after looking through my closet and declaring I have nothing to wear."

Her full lips, set in a slight pout, enticed him. "See you tomorrow." He spun on his heel and hurried toward his truck before he changed his mind and dragged her into his arms.

Slipping into his cab, he gripped the steering wheel. He hadn't thought much about the dance until now. Even if Granny had manipulated him and Jordan into taking her and Doug, this was a date in everyone's eyes—even his. The implications quaked through him. He shored up his defenses against Jordan's lure. He didn't want to be hurt a second time by her.

"Mom, why do I have to do schoolwork?" Nicholas shouted from the den where he sat at his grandmother's desk. "We have to go to the ranch in an hour."

Jordan entered the room with a refreshed glass of iced tea. "Then you have an hour to finish the essay."

"But it's Saturday."

"The beauty of homeschooling is we have the freedom to work anytime we need to."

"I hate writing."

"I know. That's why we're working on it."

"But, Mom—"

"We can skip the riding lesson today if you need more time."

"I can tell you the strengths and weaknesses of the North and South during the Civil War. I'm a lousy speller. You know how long it takes me to find a word."

"All I want is your rough draft. Then Monday we'll edit it together."

Nicholas sighed loudly, the sound expelled from his

pouting lips. And just in case she didn't hear the first one, he did it again. He stared at the computer screen and typed a few words then resumed staring.

"I'm leaving with Aunt Rachel. We're taking Granny with us shopping. Alexa has volunteered to take you with them to the ranch. I'm letting Nana know you can't go if you don't have your essay done."

Nicholas grumbled something under his breath.

Jordan decided to let it go. He did just about everything easily and well except writing. Grammar and spelling came hard to him. Putting his ideas into words on the paper was a long-drawn-out process. Like other activities involving his fine motor skills, he avoided writing if at all possible.

After Jordan told her mother about the assignment that Nicholas needed to finish, Rachel arrived to take Granny and her shopping. Their grandmother insisted on not using her walker. She did take her cane.

"My flowered dress is perfectly good for the dance." Granny sat in the back with her black purse on her lap.

"Don't you want to look your best tonight for Doug?" Rachel pulled out of the driveway.

"Nonsense. I could come in a sack and Doug wouldn't care."

"Granny, you might as well give up if you're going to cling to that attitude. Rachel is on a mission to outfit us for this dance." Jordan turned around and looked at her grandmother. "Remember this evening is your idea."

"One I'm starting to regret. All I wanted to do was get you and Zachary together."

"Granny!" Jordan mocked a severity she didn't really feel. How could she be upset when she herself was starting to want more from Zachary than friendship?

"Oh, hush, child. You knew exactly what I was up to

from the beginning. Someone had to shake some sense into that young man of yours."

"Zachary isn't my young man."

"Yes, he is. He just doesn't know it. We'll get him to see it."

"We will?" Jordan swallowed hard.

Granny waved her hand in the air. "You two were meant to be together eleven years ago, but pride and stubbornness got in the way. That needs to change. Neither one is good for a relationship. Remember I was married for thirty-seven years. Happily, I might add."

"I think Zachary might have something to say about your matchmaking."

"Child, he'll come to his senses soon enough."

Will he? Jordan remembered how he backed away the evening before. She'd been sure he was going to kiss her and he hadn't. She'd wanted him to, and when he hadn't, frustration had deluged her.

Dressed in a classic black sheath with three-inch-high heels, Jordan descended the stairs at her house on Saturday night. Her gaze connected with Zachary's as he stood at the bottom waiting for her. When he smiled, all she could think about was her senior prom and the same look of admiration that glimmered in his eyes. Her legs weakened. She gripped the railing to keep herself from melting at the heart-stopping expression on his face that for an instant wiped away eleven years. This wasn't prom—just the Alumni Homecoming Dance. They weren't teenagers in love. Sadness pricked her for a brief moment.

He held out his hand to her, and she settled hers in his. "You look beautiful."

She took in his dark Western-style suit with a black

string tie and cowboy boots. "You don't look half bad yourself."

He tipped his Stetson toward her. "Well, thank ya, ma'am."

Nicholas escorted Granny from the back of the house where her bedroom was. He grinned from ear to ear as though he held a secret no one knew.

Zachary gave Granny a wolf whistle. "You're gonna wow all the guys tonight."

A blush painted the older woman's wrinkled cheeks pink as she slowly moved forward in a floor-length royal-blue gown with long sleeves. "I bet you say that to all the gals."

"No, ma'am. Only the special ones." Zachary winked at Granny.

The color deepened on her face to a bright red. "He's a keeper, Jordan."

When the doorbell rang, Nicholas hurried toward the foyer and let Doug inside. The man dressed in a tux stared at Granny for a long moment as if no one else was around, then approached her.

Carrying a box, Doug opened it and slipped a corsage on Granny's wrist. "These roses pale in comparison to you."

A noise behind Granny intruded on the romantic moment. "Mom, I found your walker. Someone hid it under your bed." Jordan's mother rolled it toward Granny.

Her grandmother's lower lip protruded. "That someone, as you well know, was me. I'm not using it." She slid her arm through the crook of Doug's. "I can hold on to him and be perfectly fine."

"Then at least use your cane. I'll go get it for you." Jordan's mom whirled around and went in search of it.

"Let's get out of here *now*." Granny began shuffling toward the front door, dragging Doug with her.

Jordan pressed her lips together. "We'd better leave. Knowing Granny, she'll start walking toward the school if we don't get out there." Grasping her son's arms, she drew him to her and kissed his cheek. "Take care of Nana. She isn't gonna be too happy we left without the cane."

Nicholas giggled. "I'll challenge her to a game of chess and let her win tonight."

"She'll know."

"Yes, but it'll take her mind off the fact Granny is out dancing."

Hearing her mom's footsteps coming down the hall, Jordan grabbed Zachary and hurried out the entrance. When she descended the porch steps, she realized she still held Zachary's hand and started to drop it. He squeezed her fingers gently and kept the connection intact—all the way to his sister's SUV. Then he opened the front passenger door for her to slip inside. Like a date.

But this isn't a date. She had to remember that.

Granny thumped the back of the driver's seat. "Get moving, young man. Eileen's on the porch with that cane."

"Yes, ma'am." Zachary threw a glance at Jordan, a smile deep in his eyes, as he started the car. "This is gonna be an interesting evening," he whispered.

"You think?"

"What was that, young man. Speak up? I don't hear as good as I used to."

Jordan twisted around. "We were just commenting on what a fun time we're gonna have."

Granny grinned. "I intend to cut a rug, as we used to say."

An hour later, true to her word, Jordan's grandmother was out on the floor with Doug dancing. The twinkling lights and candles lent a romantic air to the evening. The music played was a combination of several decades for the alumni who attended—none Granny's but that didn't stop her, although she confined herself to slow dances.

Leaning close, Zachary handed Jordan a cup of punch and said, "I hope when I'm her age, I enjoy life half as much as your grandmother."

"Yeah, she has a unique outlook." His nearness doubled her heartbeat like the tempo of a fast song.

They had talked with several old friends, watched Granny and Doug on the floor, but he had yet to ask her to dance.

She turned toward him, using that motion to step back and give herself some breathing room. "Nicholas wanted me to ask you to Sunday dinner tomorrow night."

"He mentioned something about it being Granny's birthday."

"She doesn't believe in celebrating her birthday, so we can't mention why I'm baking a double-chocolate-fudge cake."

He tossed back his head and laughed. "So, no presents?"

"Oh, no. She's told me she's got all she needs. She doesn't want another trinket or something she would have to dust."

"Does Doug know?"

"Yes. I've invited him, but he promised no gifts."

"What time?"

"Six."

"Then I'll be there." He inched nearer, taking her elbow.

Her heartbeat pulsated a salsa. His fingers on her skin branded their imprint into her brain. Goose bumps covered her bare arms. "Remember, just a regular old family dinner."

"Yes, ma'am. I wouldn't want to be on your grandmother's bad side.

"Are you kidding? You can do no wrong."

Another slow dance began. "Let's give it a try. I hate to think an eighty-year-old woman is putting us to shame."

Jordan swallowed several times to clear the tightness in her throat. Although the leisurely rhythm vibrated through the air, her heart still picked up speed. "Are you sure?"

His gaze linked with hers. "Yes." He drew her out onto the gym floor and into his embrace. "It's been a while, but I think I remember."

As his arms wrapped around her, she'd come home. She couldn't fight her feelings any longer. She loved him. And no amount of telling herself not to was going to change that.

Zachary shouldn't have asked her to dance. That was his downfall. But he'd taken a look at her, the dim lighting adding a certain intimacy to the air, and the invitation just tumbled from his lips. Then once he'd put his arms around her, thoughts of their senior prom all those years ago attacked his defenses, tearing them down.

Tomorrow he would regret this—opening this door to the past—but for the time being he would enjoy having her close to him. Feeling her heart thumping against his chest. Touching her warmth. Smelling her vanilla scent.

When the music stopped, with all the barriers gone he framed her face in his hands and stared into her dark-chocolate gaze as though he were a teenage boy again and in love for the first time.

People left the dance floor, but he couldn't move. Transfixed by the smile that brightened her eyes, a smile that coaxed his heart to forget and forgive, he didn't want to be in the middle of a crowded gym. He wanted her alone.

With that thought in mind, he grabbed her hand and tugged her after him.

"Where are we going?"

"A surprise."

"What about Granny and Doug?"

"We'll be back before the dance is over."

He exited the building, his destination before him—a hundred yards away. Crossing the parking lot, he slowed his step to allow her to keep up. When he reached the gate to the football stadium, he punched in a code and opened it.

"How do you know how to get inside?"

"I've helped Coach out some in the past, and he hasn't changed it in the last few years. Probably a quarter of the town knows how to get in here." Zachary mounted the steps to the stands and stopped when he reached the row right under the press box. "Remember?"

"Yes, this is where you asked me to go steady." Her words came out in a breathless, halting gush.

Whether from his fast pace or from something else, he didn't know. For the evening he wanted to forget all his fear and doubts and just enjoy her company—like in the past.

He pulled her down next to him on the bench, slung his arm around her shoulders and pressed her against his side. "This used to be my favorite place. My thinking place."

"It's not anymore?"

"No. Now I usually just go riding."

She shivered.

"Cold."

"A little."

He shrugged out of his coat and gave it to her.

"Thanks." She snuggled into its warmth.

And he wanted his arms around her—not his coat. He

stared at the dark field below then lifted his gaze to the nearly full moon in the clear sky. Its radiance gave them enough light to see by. He inhaled a deep breath of the recently mowed grass. Silence surrounded them, except that his heartbeat throbbed in his ears, drowning out all common sense.

He shouldn't be here with Jordan.

He should leave—he shifted toward her. Their gazes bound across the few inches that separated them. His throat went dry. Thoughts fled his mind. His blood rushed to his limbs.

He leaned closer and brushed his lips across hers. Drawing her totally to him, he fenced her against him and deepened the kiss until he became lost in the sensations bombarding him—her heady scent, the feel of her mouth on his, the little gasp of surprise that had come from her when he first made a tactile connection.

When he pulled back slightly, she murmured, "Why did you kiss me?"

"Can you deny you haven't thought about how it would be after all these years?"

"Is that all it was to you? A way to satisfy an itch?"

Her questions sobered him—propelled him into the present. He shouldn't have kissed her. Too much stood between them. He rose. "We'd better get back. I wouldn't want your grandmother to worry."

She removed his suit jacket and thrust it into his hands. "I don't need this anymore." Whirling around, she started for the aisle.

He let her go, following a few paces behind her. Her stiff arms at her sides and long strides announced to the world she was upset.

Just friends. There could be no in between for them. Friends only.

Okay, so now that he'd gotten the kiss out of his system, he could move forward. Cement his relationship with Nicholas and keep Jordan at arm's length.

Yeah, right.

Nicholas opened the front door. "Dad, you're here. Mom said you might not come."

"Sure. When does a guy turn down a home-cooked meal?" Sunday evening Zachary stepped through the threshold into the best-smelling house on the planet.

Aromas of baking bread, pot roast and spices assailed his nostrils. Mingling among those smells he caught a whiff of coffee. His stomach roiled, protesting his hunger. He'd worked nonstop from right after church to thirty minutes ago. He refused to let the previous night intrude into his thoughts, but if he stopped for any amount of time, he began to think about the kiss.

He followed his son into the den and found Granny, Doug, Eileen, Rachel and Jordan sitting and talking. Everyone stopped and stared at him when he came into the room.

Awkward, he covered the distance to Granny and presented her with a bouquet of flowers. "For the prettiest gal here."

A flush stained her cheeks, much like it did Jordan's. "Who told you it was my birthday? Nicholas?"

His son shook his head.

Her sharp gaze landed on Jordan. "You?"

"Yes, and I made you a chocolate cake. If you don't watch out, I'll put eighty-one candles on it."

"Not unless you want to call the fire department, child."

Jordan stared at Zachary. "What about 'Don't bring a gift' did you not understand?"

He slunk to the nearest chair and plopped down onto it. "I didn't think flowers would be considered a birthday present."

"Dear, why don't you want to celebrate your birthday?" Doug looked at Granny. His white mustache framed his pinched lips.

"Because I've given them up. I did when I turned sixty."

"What if I said I picked these from Becca's garden?" Zachary still held the bouquet in his hand.

Jordan stood and took the flowers from him. "I didn't know your sister has a rose garden."

"She doesn't. The only one she has is a vegetable garden," he said in a low voice for her ears only.

"Well, since he went to the trouble to get them, you might as well stick them in some water and put them in the dining room. And I thank you kindly, Zachary." Granny angled toward Doug on the couch next to her, plastered her biggest smile on her face, her wrinkles deepening, and patted his hand between them. "Your presence is all I need on my birthday."

Zachary surged to his feet. "I'll help you, Jordan."

In the kitchen, he blew a breath out between pursed lips. "I messed up."

"No, you didn't. Granny loves flowers, but she couldn't make a big deal out of it because she has insisted for years nothing special on her birthday."

"Where did Nicholas disappear to?"

She waved her hand toward the kitchen door. "He's out back with his cousins. Taylor's helping him fix the fence where Tucker keeps digging out of the yard."

"Beagles love to escape. I had one when I was a boy that was a master at climbing the fence. Tucker did like the ranch, especially the squirrels and birds he ended up chasing around."

After filling a glass vase with water, Jordan put the yellow roses into it one by one. "Dinner is about ready."

"Can I set the table?"

"Done, but you can put these flowers on the sideboard in the dining room." She held the vase toward him.

He clasped it, their fingers brushing against each other. He locked his gaze on hers, and all the sensations from the night before when he'd embraced her, kissed her, washed through him anew. He jerked back as though shocked by their touch. The glass vase crashed to the tile floor, shattering between them, shards flying everywhere.

"I'm sorry. I didn't mean to pull back." Staring down at the mess, he almost didn't hear her reply.

"Yes, you did. What's going on between us?" She dragged the trash can to the broken vase and stooped down to pick up the pieces.

Bending down next to her, he helped clean up the mess. "Nothing."

"Oh, I see. That kiss meant nothing to you."

"I shouldn't have done that. I got caught up in the moment, remembering the time when I had asked you to go steady sitting in that very spot."

Emotions—hurt, sadness and finally irritation—flitted across her features. Her eyes downcast, she continued to work, but he'd seen the misty look in them.

He seized her wrist. "I made this mess. I'll take care of it. You get dinner on the table. Where's your broom and dustpan?"

"That's okay. I'd rather you go get Nicholas and the other kids. I need space." She compressed her mouth into a thin line, but her eyes still glistened.

"Fine." He rose and headed toward the back door.

Space was a good thing. Because for a few seconds, he'd wanted to sweep her into his arms and take away that hurt look inching back into her expression. But he couldn't. He'd loved two women in his life and had discovered he couldn't trust either one not to trample his heart. His fiancée had walked away after his bull-riding injury. And he'd been left alone with his grief—again.

Between Jordan and Audrey, he'd decided to live a life without emotional entanglements. Much easier on him— until Jordan turned up again.

"Do you want to go out and look at the stars with me?" Nicholas asked Zachary after the dishes were done that evening.

"Sure."

"How about you, Mom? The moon is full. You'll be able to see the craters."

Jordan put the dish towel over the handle on the stove. "I don't—"

"Please. We should be able to see Venus, too."

"Okay. For a few minutes."

Out on the deck, Nicholas removed the covering over his telescope and began adjusting it to view the moon.

"Nicholas, can you come in and help me with something?" Granny stood at the kitchen door, her expression hidden in the shadows.

"Yes. I'll be back. I think it's set up." He pointed up into the sky to the left. "Venus is that way. Low on the horizon." As he hurried away, her grandmother backed away to allow Nicholas inside.

The click of the door resonated in the quiet. Jordan peered at the telescope then Zachary. "You go first."

While she waited for her turn, music drifted outside from an open upstairs window in her son's room. Words from "Sealed with a Kiss" sounded, competing with Tucker's howl.

Zachary straightened and glanced toward the window. "What's that?"

"Granny has a CD with love songs on it that she plays occasionally."

In the light that streamed from the kitchen Zachary's forehead creased. "Isn't that our son's room?"

"Yes. He's at it again with some help from Granny."

"It's in His Kiss" followed next.

He burst out laughing. "What's next? 'Then I Kissed Her'?"

"Actually I think 'Something's Gotta Hold of My Heart.'"

"Yeah, heartburn."

Jordan chuckled, catching sight of Nicholas peeking out the kitchen window with Granny next to him. "Don't look now but they are spying on us."

He grabbed her and drew her to him. "Are you game for a little fun?"

"What?"

Her pulse thudded against her neck. He plastered her against him, then dipped her backward while he planted a kiss on her mouth. Her head spun, especially when he came up, dragging her with him. Dots before her eyes danced to the rhythm of the music.

"Do you think those two are still looking?" he said against her lips, his warm breath caressing them.

She leaned back and glanced up. "Yep. now they're blatantly standing in the window."

Zachary pivoted around, shoved his hands to his hips and asked, "What do you think you're doing?"

Nicholas stuck his head out the kitchen door. "Granny wanted to hear her CD."

Jordan stepped around Zachary. "She might but the whole neighborhood doesn't need to be serenaded. Nor do we. Close your window and get ready for bed."

"Ah, Mom."

"It's getting late and there's no more entertainment out here for you to see." She crossed her arms to emphasize the point.

Evidently Nicholas decided not to argue, but instead did as she asked.

"Someone needs to talk to him." Zachary raked his hand through his hair. "He needs to understand about our relationship." Again his fingers combed their way through his dark strands.

Explain it to me. She clamped her lips together to still those words. "Then I suggest you have a father-son talk with him."

His eyes widened. "You don't want to do it?"

"I don't think I could explain it well." *Since you're sending me mixed messages.*

"Okay, I'll tuck him in tonight and have that talk. I'll take care of everything."

"You do that." Jordan marched toward the back door and entered the kitchen, not caring if Zachary followed her or not.

He was going to hurt her and there was nothing she could do about it. She'd had her chance years ago and Zachary wasn't going to give her a second one—no matter how sorry she was concerning not telling him about Nicholas.

Chapter Ten

Half an hour later Zachary sat on Nicholas's bed, staring at his son's expectant face. Zachary gulped. He'd only been a father for less than a month. He wasn't ready for a father-son talk about the opposite sex, even if it had only to do with him and Jordan. When he thought about it, he'd probably never be.

"Nicholas, your mother and I are only friends."

"I saw you kiss her."

"I was playing with you." And shouldn't have done it. What was it about being around Jordan that made him forget his common sense?

"Why can't you two marry?"

"Marriage is serious and can't be taken lightly." *You have to trust each other.* But he couldn't say that to his son.

"I'm not. I want us to be a family."

"We are a family. You'll always be our son."

"That's not what I meant." Nicholas frowned, folding his arms over his stomach.

"I know. Your mother loves you and I do, too."

"But you don't love each other?"

He wanted to say no, but the word lodged in his throat. He swallowed hard, but the lump was immovable. "I'll always care about her," he finally murmured.

His son's frown evolved into a scowl. "That's not…" He pulled his cover up to his shoulder and twisted away. "Oh, never mind."

"Good night, son." Zachary bent forward and kissed him on his side of his head.

When Zachary descended the stairs a minute later, he found Jordan sitting on the bottom one, her head hanging down, her hands loosely clasped between her legs. He settled beside her. "I told him, or rather I tried to."

"I heard."

"You listened?"

She slanted a look at him. "I'll have to pick up the pieces after you leave. I needed to know what you two talked about."

"What a pair we make. Suspicious of each other."

"You don't know Nicholas like I do."

He surged to his feet, curling and uncurling his hands. He didn't like all these emotions flooding him. Life was simpler when he didn't feel so intensely. "And whose fault is that?" His hurried strides chewed up the distance to the front door. Out on the porch, he paused, tried to compose himself. Couldn't.

On the long drive to his ranch his gut kicked like a bucking horse. How was he supposed to forgive Jordan for robbing him of ten years with his child? The only one he'd ever have? He'd missed so much already. Every time he was with Nicholas that was reinforced. And yet, she'd tried to tell him once—thought she'd been rejected by him. What a pair they were!

When he drove down the gravel road that led to his place, he saw the light in Becca's kitchen still on. He swerved his truck and parked behind her house. He didn't want to be alone with his thoughts. She'd been there after his rodeo accident and helped him adjust.

He knocked on the door, and a few seconds later it was opened by his older sister. He tried to smile a greeting, but it died instantly on his lips.

"Your dinner at Jordan's didn't go well?"

He shook his head. "Nicholas keeps trying to fix us up." He trudged into the kitchen and sank into a chair at the table.

"Ah, that's cute."

"No, it isn't."

"Why not? You loved Jordan once."

His gut constricted even more. "It's not that simple."

Becca sat across from him. "I feel bad about not saying something directly to you about her calling eleven years ago. If I had, this would be a moot point."

"It's not your fault."

"I can understand why you're angry with her, but you've gotta let it go. It will eat you up inside. Color your relationship with your son."

"How's this any different than if we were married and divorced?" He set his elbows on the table and steepled his fingers.

"It's isn't really. Most children want to see their divorced parents back together."

"I think Granny is encouraging him to get us together. Actually there is no 'think' about it. I know."

"Knowing Jordan's grandmother, you aren't gonna change her mind. She's like a pit bull. She isn't gonna let it go."

He rubbed his hands down his face. "I'm gonna have to stay away as much as possible."

"How's that gonna help you get to know your son better?"

"I thought I'd have Nicholas go camping with us next weekend. Getting away from Tallgrass will be good."

"You mean running away. Your problems won't disappear. Face them. As a teenager, you had deep feelings for Jordan."

Zachary pushed to his feet. "Yeah, a long time ago. Not now. The best we can be is friends for Nicholas's sake." If he said it enough, he would come to believe it.

He strode from his sister's place and headed toward his own. Answers still eluded him like the grand prize now in a rodeo competition. When he pulled up in front, he stared at his dark house. Once he'd dreamed of having a home full of children, a loving relationship—with Jordan. Then when that blew up in his face, he slowly rebuilt his dream with Audrey, who had left him because he couldn't be the father of the children she'd wanted. There wouldn't be a third time.

At least I have one son. Thank You, Lord, for that.

Early before dawn the next morning after Zachary had called Jordan, Nicholas rushed into the barn. "Has Buttercup had the foal yet?"

With his hands clasped, his forearms on the stall door, Zachary peered toward Nicholas and her coming toward him. "Nope. But she's getting close."

"Can I see? Can I see?" Nicholas hopped up and down.

Zachary passed Jordan going to the tack room. "I'll be right back."

After the evening she and Zachary had, the timing of the birth of the foal wasn't good. During the middle of her sleepless night, she'd come to a decision. If being his friend was the only relationship she could have with Zachary, she would try to make it work. Which meant she had to tamp down her feelings for him. He'd broken her heart once before. She rubbed her hand over her chest. She was afraid that it was too late this time, as well. It hurt to be in love with a man who didn't feel the same.

"Here, son, use this." Zachary put a stool in front of the stall door.

"Can't we go inside?"

"I don't like to unless there's a problem."

Zachary stood on the left side of Nicholas while she took up her post on the right.

Nicholas squealed. "Look. I see a leg."

Seeing the joy and wonder on her son's face made the uncomfortable feeling okay. She would do anything for Nicholas.

"If you decide to be a vet, you could work with large animals. There are plenty of ranches around here." Zachary's gaze slipped from their son to Jordan. The tired lines about Zachary's eyes underscored his sleepless night, too.

Groans from the mare filled the air. Jordan thought about when she'd had Nicholas, alone because he was a few weeks early. Zachary had been on the other side of the world, oblivious to the fact he was becoming a father. As though he were thinking the same thing, his lips disappeared beneath his tight expression. He turned away, keeping his full attention on the drama occurring in the stall.

"Guys, the head is out." Nicholas pointed at the dark, wet foal.

The mare strained, her stomach rising and falling. Buttercup struggled to her feet, twirled around, then plopped down on the hay-covered floor.

Nicholas's eyes grew huge. "Is everything okay?"

"Yeah, she's doing fine. The foal's coming out the right way. Sometimes the mama gets a little restless, impatient."

Like a lot of mamas around the world. But she kept that to herself, not wanting to remind Zachary he hadn't been at his son's birth.

When the baby came completely out, Nicholas jumped up and down, clapping his hands. "This cinches it. I want to be a vet. I'm going to have to really get into science now. When we get home today, let's work on that first."

"First, we're going over your essay. Then we can do science. Your anatomy class with Dr. Reynolds should be helpful."

"We're studying the heart and its function right now. I already knew quite a bit because of my problem. I've read a lot about it."

Jordan captured Zachary's look, trying to gauge his reaction to his son's words. His closed expression told her nothing of what was going on inside him until his jaw twitched.

"I thought this next weekend you could go camping with me and Aunt Becca's family. Would you be interested, Nicholas?"

Her son whirled around on the stool, nearly toppling over. After steadying himself, he radiated his joy. "I've always wanted to go camping. When?"

"We'll leave Saturday morning and come back Sunday evening."

"Mom?"

She wished she'd had some warning about this. Biting down on the inside of her mouth, she kept the first words that came to mind inside. After last night she didn't need any more tension between her and Zachary. "That sounds fine to me," she finally said when her son gave her a quizzical look.

"Mom, you should go, too. We've never been camping."

With the bugs and snakes? Her idea of roughing it was a two-star hotel. "I don't know."

"Please. It will be fun."

It is if you like to get dirty and sleep on the ground. She peered at Zachary, who remained stony quiet. When she swept her attention back to Nicholas, he studied them, his expression hovering somewhere between a grin and a frown. "I'll have to think about it, but that doesn't mean you can't go, hon."

The foal finally made it to its wobbly legs while Buttercup licked the baby. When it started nursing, Nicholas hopped down. "Can I go in now?"

"Sure, but don't interfere with the foal nursing." Zachary opened the stall door.

"I won't. I know how important it is for the mama and baby to bond."

Nicholas moved in slow motion inside, his eyes as round as wagon wheels while he took everything in. He began talking softly to the two animals. The mother's ears cocked toward him.

Zachary's hand clamped around hers, and he tugged her back toward the middle of the barn. "You can come if you want, but unless you've made an about-face on the idea of camping, you'd be miserable."

"Is that why you planned the outing? To exclude me?"

"No, I just want to get to know my son. I'm having to make up for lost time. When he talks about his heart defect, he's so matter-of-fact, but it couldn't have been easy. I wish I could have been there for him, held his hand, let him know I loved him."

Tears gathered in her eyes. "Are you ever going to forgive me?"

"That's what the Lord wants." He dropped his hand away from hers—sadness shadowing his eyes. "I'm really trying, Jordan, to do what's right."

But he hadn't forgiven her yet. He'd all but said that. His unspoken intent hurt more than she wanted to acknowledge. She saw out of the corner of her eye Nicholas watching them. She stepped closer, Zachary's male scent vying with the odors of the barn—horse, hay, dust. Tilting her chin, she averted her head so her son couldn't see her expression. "So am I, Zachary." She sucked in a stabilizing breath. "And I haven't changed that much. I'm still not gung-ho about camping."

"Well, that's reassuring. Not everything has changed." He strode toward Nicholas.

"Child, what are you doing here? You should be getting ready to go camping with Nicholas and Zachary." Granny shuffled into the kitchen not a half an hour after dawn peeked over the horizon on Saturday morning.

Jordan nursed a large cup of strong coffee. She hadn't slept a wink last night. Each time she'd started to nod off, visions of her lying on the ground with bugs and spiders and snakes crawling all over her intruded. The picture destroyed her peace.

"I'm not wanted," she said in a self-pitying tone that even made her hunch her shoulders.

"Oh, my, you've got it bad. You're too busy feeling sorry for yourself. If you want the young man, you need to get up and do something about it. Sitting here moping won't change the circumstances." Granny eased down beside her and took her hand. "When you were a teenager, you still had a—" she thought for a few seconds "—a lot of growing up to do. You were used to getting your way, especially with Zachary. You thought you could go away for a couple of years and come back here after you'd done what you wanted and pick right up where you two left off."

"No, I didn't...." Yes, secretly she had thought that. She'd wanted to go away to see what was out there and art school in Savannah gave her the means. She'd been eighteen and not ready to settle down even in a year like Zachary had thought. "Okay, maybe I did."

"But Zachary didn't stay here waiting for you. And when you found that out, you were hurt and angry. Then Nicholas had problems, and you had your hands full. You grew up fast. You aren't that same young girl, and Zachary isn't that same young man. Get out there and get to know him in his element. Go camping. Your son asked you again before he left to go spend the night at the ranch. Give you three a chance."

Jordan pulled her hand free and wrapped her fingers around the warm mug, drawing in the fragrance of the coffee. The best smell in the world. "I'm not the one who's fighting us being together as a family."

"Do you blame Zachary? You can be so stubborn at times." Her grandmother snorted unladylike. "To paraphrase the words of one of my favorite Gene Pitney songs, 'only love has the power to fix a broken heart.' Give him a reason to fall in love with you again."

"But he doesn't trust me."

"When he does love you, his trust will come." Granny struggled to her feet, steadied herself by gripping the table's edge. "I took the liberty of borrowing Doug's sleeping bag and small pup tent. In the hallway by the front door. Now get before they leave without you."

Her grandmother was right. She would have to fight for Zachary's love. She'd learned to fight when Nicholas got so sick. Jumping up, she kissed Granny on the cheek and hurried toward her bedroom.

Zachary leaned against the fence of his largest corral and watched Nicholas, on the back of Chief, gallop to one end, round the barrel and race back to the other one making a figure eight. His son was improving every day.

Nicholas trotted to him. "I did it."

When he held his hand up, Zachary gave him a high five. "Let's try it one more time before we leave for Prairie Lake."

"May I take my rope with us? I'd like to practice while we're camping."

"Sounds good to me. The HHH Junior Rodeo is only a few weeks away. Practice is the key to getting better."

"Maybe I'll rope a bear."

Zachary laughed. "I hope not. But maybe a tree stump."

Nicholas maneuvered his horse around so he could start the run again. He nudged the gelding.

As his son shot forward, the sound of a car pulling up drifted to Zachary. He glanced sideways and tensed. What was Jordan doing here? Turning back toward Nicholas, he prepared himself for a confrontation over the fact their son was racing around a set of barrels.

He heard her approach. The hairs on his nape stood up. He stiffened as he pushed off, his fingers grasping the wooden slat. She stopped right behind him on the other side. A fence between them. A past between them—a past he kept dredging up.

Nicholas finished his figure eight. "Hi, Mom. What are you doing here?"

"I decided to take your father's invitation up and come camping with you all."

Zachary strode to the gate and opened it for Nicholas to leave the corral.

"That's great!" His son loped toward the entrance to the barn and dismounted.

"Is the invitation still open?" Jordan came up to Zachary as he latched the gate.

No, I didn't mean it. I need to stay away from you. You're too tempting. Zachary pivoted and faced her, forcing a smile to his lips. "Sure. You do understand we'll be outdoors with everything you get squeamish about?"

"If Nicholas enjoys it, I want to be able to share it with him."

"Suit yourself. You were warned."

Her eyes became round, her eyebrows raised. "It's just a few bugs."

"Yeah, just a few," he murmured and started for the barn.

She hurried after him. "Nicholas is riding well."

"Yes. I told you I wouldn't have him do anything he's not ready for. You need to trust me on that."

She grasped his arm and stopped him. When he glanced back at her, she asked, "Is that a two-way street?"

Trust didn't come easily to him anymore, partially because of this woman who moved to stand in front of him.

"Zachary, I know you have a good reason to be leery of me, but we both have our son's well-being in mind."

"So I should trust you, no questions asked, because of Nicholas?"

She lifted her chin. "Yes."

He shook free. "We need to meet Becca at her house in twenty minutes."

He continued his path toward Nicholas cooling down his gelding. *It's gonna be a long weekend, trying to avoid*

Jordan. I thought I could be friends with her and not care beyond that. But I don't think that's possible.

Jordan plopped down on a fallen log by a stream that fed into Prairie Lake, not far from their campsite. If she didn't know better, she was sure that Zachary picked the most primitive area for them to set up camp. And then on top of that, he'd insisted she put up her own tent as the others were doing. She had—or at least she thought it would stay up even if it did lean a little to the left.

She wouldn't say a word. She was determined to do this with a smile on her face.

A whiff of grilled hamburgers wafted to her. Her stomach rumbled. She rose and gathered up her bundle of firewood and headed toward the sound of voices through the trees.

"I caught a fish today." Nicholas ran over to her and held up his hands to indicate a foot. "I threw it back, but I enjoyed fishing. Dad said tomorrow we can go early in the morning and will probably catch a lot more."

"That's great, hon. I hope this will be enough wood." Jordan dumped her armful onto the pile not far from the fire pit.

"So long as we have a big enough fire to last the whole night, we should be fine." Zachary clamped his lips together.

"Fine? What do you mean? It shouldn't get too cold with our sleeping bags." Jordan dusted off her jeans.

"I'm not talking about the cold. It's for the bears, bobcats and coyotes."

"Bears? Bobcats…" Her voice faded as a twinkle danced in Zachary's eyes. She punched him in the arm. "Funny. So what's the fire really for?"

"We're gonna roast marshmallows and tell scary stories," Nicholas piped in and returned to Becca.

"I know I'm not much of a nature buff, but I can tell scary stories. You're not gonna sleep at all tonight." She winked at Zachary and sauntered past him to help Becca with dinner.

"We'll just see who's up the whole night, too scared to sleep," he said behind her with a chuckle.

She was afraid it might be her. Not that she would let Zachary know she didn't get any sleep.

After helping Becca with the dinner, Jordan sat down with her plate, piled high with a thick, juicy hamburger, baked beans, macaroni and cheese and cole slaw. The heat from the fire that Zachary and Paul, Becca's husband, had built warmed her. Now that the sun had disappeared behind the tall pines, scrub oaks and hackberry trees, the temperature had dropped a few degrees.

"How early are you and Nicholas going fishing tomorrow morning?" Jordan asked when Zachary took a seat near her.

"Crack of dawn."

"That early?" Who was she kidding? She wouldn't probably close her eyes all night so why not get up and join them. "I'd like to go with you two. Is anyone else coming?"

"Nope. Paul and I have a challenge going. He has a favorite fishing hole and I have one. We're gonna see who can get the most. He's taking his boys."

"Then I'll even out the numbers. Three to three."

His brow wrinkled, he looked sideways at her. "Then you want to fish?"

"Why not? If you and Nicholas are gonna, I might as well try."

"You'll bait your own hook?"

"Fine. Isn't it just rubbery things?"

He grinned. "Live worms. They come in dirt."

"I know how worms come."

"Just wanted you to know all the details."

"Okay, so I'm a girly girl."

His smile broadened, reaching deep into his eyes. "I've been impressed so far."

"Yeah, well, wait. It isn't totally dark yet."

His robust laugh echoed through the woods encircling them, bouncing off objects and returning to enclose them in an intimacy. For just a moment. "We still have the scary stories," he said, cutting through the emotion-packed tension.

"I have a better idea." Jordan turned to the rest of them around the fire. "Why don't we play charades?"

"Yeah, I like that game," Ashley said opposite Jordan.

"I'm good at it." Nicholas jumped to his feet and threw his plate away, then grabbed a brownie.

Zachary rubbed his chin. "That's actually a good suggestion. Charades it is."

An hour later with darkness surrounding them like a black curtain and their stomachs full of chocolate and marshmallows, the fire the only bright spot, Jordan sat with Becca and Ashley across from Zachary, Mike, Cal and Nicholas. Paul held the tin container out for Jordan to draw her final selection for charades. She read it and gulped then handed it to Paul, who showed it to the guy team.

She unfolded her hands to resemble a book then turned her hand in a full circle.

"A book and movie," Becca shouted.

She held up seven fingers, then indicated the second word. Without roaring, she gave a fierce face and acted as if she pounced on prey.

"Bobcat," Zachary said with a laugh.

Swinging around, she glared at him.

Becca snapped her fingers. "Lion."

Ashley bounced up and down on her seat. "Oh, oh. It's *The Lion, the Witch and the Wardrobe*."

"Yes!" Jordan high-fived Ashley. "Way to go."

Next Zachary stood, groaned when he read his pick, *The Princess Diaries,* then faced his team to begin. He started to do something, scowled then walked to Paul and whispered something to him. "Ah, okay," Zachary said and came back to the center.

He pantomimed it was a movie and three words. He paused, thought a few seconds then pranced around the fire as though he wore high heels, then eased daintily into a chair. His team looked at him as if he were crazy.

For the next few minutes Zachary tried to coax the title out of the three boys. When he opened his hand like a book and pretended to write in it, Nicholas finally said, "Journal."

Zachary smacked his palms together and shouted, "Close."

"Hey, no talking." Jordan pointed toward Zachary. "That should be a thirty-second penalty."

"Time, without even adding a penalty. Girls win three to two."

Mike stuck out his chest, a pout on his face. "We had harder ones. That's the only reason you all won."

"Mike, they won fair and square." Paul put the tin container back with the other dishes. "It's bedtime. We need to get up early tomorrow. Got a challenge to win."

After standing, Jordan stretched and rolled her head to ease her tight muscles. Exhausted, she covered her open mouth. "I don't think I'm gonna have any trouble sleeping tonight."

"Well, don't let the bed bugs bite." Zachary winked and headed with Nicholas to the tent they were sharing.

Jordan watched everyone scatter to their respective tents. How did she get stuck by herself? *'Cause you don't belong. This is Zachary's family, not yours.*

Flipping back the flap, she crawled inside the small space where she would sleep. After snuggling into the warmth of her bag, Zachary's comment about the bed bugs came back to haunt her. She switched on her flashlight and checked everywhere around her for any sign of an insect or any other creepy, crawling critters. When she thought it was safe, she relaxed and zipped herself in.

That was when the sounds intruded. The constant chatter of the crickets with an occasional bullfrog taunted her with the idea of sleep—just out of her reach. She stared into the darkness. The hoot of an owl nearby made her gasp. She hunkered down into her bag and squeezed her eyes closed. Sleep finally descended when she relaxed her tense muscles enough to allow it in.

Only to be jerked wide-awake by a howl. She bolted upright, flinging her arms out, connecting with the side of the tent. Canvas swallowed her in its clutches, trying to smother her rather than shelter her. Trapped. With a shudder, she squirmed in her sleeping bag, fighting with the zipper while shoving at the walls of the tent that had fallen on her. Twisting to the side, she searched for an opening and rolled down a small incline, ending up at the bottom in a tangle.

Her heartbeat thundered so loud in her ears she barely heard Zachary call her name. Then suddenly he freed her from the canvas and knelt down next to her.

"What happened, Jordan?"

"My zipper is stuck," she said between pants. She needed to get out of the confining sleeping bag.

He placed a calming hand on her. "Let me."

Five seconds later he liberated her totally. She sat up and inhaled deeply of the oxygen-rich air. Another howl reverberated through the woods. "What's that?" She threw herself into his strong arms.

For a moment he held her before saying, "It's a coyote." He helped her up, stooped and grabbed the tent and bedding. "We're safe."

"How do you know that?"

"I've been camping here many times and a coyote hasn't bothered me yet."

"There's always a first time." The trembling in her hands quickly overtook her whole body.

He tossed the items on the ground not too far from the fire then drew her into his embrace again. "You're all right."

She laid her head against his chest, feeling the steady beating of his heart beneath her ear. "You said a coyote hasn't bothered you. Has something else?"

"Raccoons. That's why our food is locked away in the car."

"Oh." Although she didn't want to encounter a raccoon, it sounded better than a coyote. From the dim light of the dying fire, she noticed the time on her watch was four in the morning. Even though her body didn't feel like it, she'd gotten a few hours of sleep. "I think I'm done for the night."

"Dawn is still a couple of hours away."

"I know but I'm not wrestling with my tent again."

"I can stay out here. Why don't you sleep with Nicholas?"

"You'd sleep out in the open?" His warmth encircled her and lured her into a serenity she wished she could maintain.

"I've done it before." His fingers skimmed down her spine.

She pressed closer. The thumping of his heartbeat increased. A sudden intake of air attested to her effect on him. She smiled. Hope blossomed within her and spread through her.

He stepped back. "I'll use this sleeping bag. You can use mine. That way we won't disturb Nicholas."

Still keyed up with her fight with her tent, she moved toward the glowing embers of the fire and sat. "I might take you up on it, but right now I can't sleep a wink."

He sank into a lawn chair nearby. "I probably can't, either."

"Ha! We have something in common."

His chuckles tickled down her spine like the feel of his fingers seconds ago. "Besides Nicholas. Yeah, I guess we do."

"Well, certainly not camping. I suck at it."

"Nicholas is having a good time."

"That's your genes. Not mine."

"But studying and the love of books are yours."

"He's a little bit of both of us and a whole lot of his own."

Zachary crossed his right arm over his chest while stroking his chin with his left hand. "Aren't most children?"

"Probably. I'd love to find out. I never pictured being a mother of one child. Growing up I enjoyed my relationship with my sister." The second she admitted that to Zachary she chanced a peek at his face.

His earlier neutral expression morphed into a frown, the cleft in his chin prominent.

"How about you? You were engaged once. Did you two talk about having a family?"

He blinked. The silence stretched between them.

"I'm sorry. I had no right to ask." What had happened to Zachary from the time she'd left to when she'd come back to Tallgrass?

"Yeah, I wanted a family. Being around my nephews and niece made me realize that."

"That's the way I feel about Rachel's family. Every year she and Mom would drive across country and visit Nicholas and I for a couple of weeks. We spent time at the beach, seeing the sights. The time we went to Jamestown and Williamsburg was so much fun. Nicholas was four. Before he got so sick he couldn't go far from home. I think that trip sparked his love of history."

Zachary's intense gaze trapped hers. "At four?"

"He was reading by three, calculating addition, subtraction and even multiplication in his head."

"What an unusual son we have."

For a long moment a bond sprang up between them. He'd roped her as if he'd taken her into his arms again. She wished he would.

Finally he turned his head, poking the fire with a stick they'd roasted marshmallows on. "What happened when he got sick?"

"His health began to deteriorate until finally his doctor heard his heart murmur and referred us to a pediatric cardiologist. They put a catheter in to repair the hole. It's like a plug. But it became infected and they had to repair it surgically. He almost died. It took quite a toll on him." *And me, but my son's alive through the grace and power of the Lord.*

He folded both arms over his chest. "I wish I could have been there for him."

"I wish you'd been there, too." It should have been that way. If only… The brief connection she'd experienced with Zachary came crashing down about her. Her memories and emotions—mostly sadness—swamped her, sagging her shoulders. She pushed to her feet. "I think I can sleep now."

As she made her way to the tent where Nicholas was, Zachary's continued silence emphasized the distance between them. She wanted his forgiveness and trust. Neither of which she had. If she ever wanted that family she'd told him she wanted, she needed to move on. Why hadn't she while she lived in South Carolina? Her excuse had always been Nicholas. But now that she was back in Tallgrass she realized it was because she'd never stopped loving Zachary, even when she'd felt rejected by him.

When she settled next to Nicholas, weariness surrounded her like the sleeping bag. But Zachary's distinctive male scent ridiculed her thoughts of slumber.

Nicholas chattered most of the way back to the ranch from the lake the next evening. Zachary tried to follow what his son said, but his mind was filled with images from the weekend camping trip. Lying in the sleeping bag where Jordan had been moments before—her vanilla fragrance taunting him. Her trying to bait her hook with a wiggly worm. Her glee at reeling in a fish only to have to throw it back because of its small size. The sleepy-eyed look she'd given him that morning when she'd crawled out of the tent behind Nicholas.

And if truth be known, he'd enjoyed himself and believed she had, too. What would it have been like if he'd known about his son from the very beginning? Would they have a parcel of kids by now? Would he have become a bull rider? Had the rodeo accident? That day changed so much for him. His career was over. His fiancée walked away because he couldn't give her what she wanted—a family. *Like Jordan wants.*

The thought she wanted more kids marked his heart like a branding iron used on horses. It was too late for him but not her. Even if he could put aside his mistrust, how could he ask her to give him a second chance when he couldn't give her any more children?

"Dad?"

"Huh?"

"Who's that at Aunt Becca's?"

Zachary swept his attention toward the blue house as he passed it. Stiffening, he sucked in a sharp breath. "My parents." He'd avoided having any real conversation with his mother about Nicholas and what had happened eleven years ago. He should have known she wouldn't be put off for long.

He slid his gaze toward Jordan in the front seat. Her ashen features spoke of her own turmoil at his parents' visit.

Chapter Eleven

When Zachary pulled up behind his parents' car, Jordan sank lower in the seat, her hands clenched beside her. *What do I say to the woman who kept my calls from Zachary, Lord? Things would be so different if she hadn't.*

"They're my grandparents?" Nicholas pushed open the back door of the truck and jumped down. Without waiting for a reply to his question, he darted across the yard toward them.

Zachary sent her a look full of concern. "I can understand if you'd rather not talk with my mom."

"I imagine she's not too happy with me, and I'm certainly not with her." Jordan stared out the windshield at her son, who embraced his grandparents as though he'd known them all his life. Didn't he realize that woman was the reason he didn't know about his father?

"She shouldn't have kept the message from me, but she was doing what mothers do—protecting their children."

She knew she wasn't being fair but the past month had been hard for her, her son and Zachary. Yes, she was to blame as well as his mother, but she'd been young, hardly an adult thrust into an adult situation she didn't know how to handle. "So you can forgive her but not me?" Finally she swung her full attention toward Zachary, narrowing her eyes when she saw the deep furrows on his forehead, the muscle in his cheek twitch, the flare of his nostrils.

His grip on the steering wheel whitened his knuckles. "You can't compare apples to oranges. The two situations are not the same."

"Yes, I can. She lied to me." Jordan shoved open the door. "It seems to me you have a double standard. I'm getting my car and leaving. I'll stop by and get Nicholas. He needs to go home. He's had a long, tiring weekend."

She started for the barn where she'd left her car parked and had only taken a few steps before Zachary blocked her path. "Nicholas can stay the night with me. He needs to spend some time with his grandparents."

Moving into his personal space, she shoved her face close to his. "No. He can visit tomorrow after he's rested and done his schoolwork."

His glare drilled through her. "I'll bring him home early tomorrow afternoon. This isn't a request. He's my son, too."

The stubborn set to his jaw declared his intention to fight for Nicholas to stay and frankly at the moment she was exhausted from the weekend's ups and downs. Her anger and energy siphoned from her. She stepped back. "Fine, but I need him home by noon. He has his anatomy class tomorrow at one."

Skirting around him, she marched down the road toward the barn. Pinpricks ran down her spine. She wouldn't look back at Zachary. She didn't need to see that he watched her.

"Mom said you're upset." Rachel came into the kitchen where Jordan was working on her laptop the next morning.

She twisted toward her older sister. "Zachary's mother is at the ranch."

"And Nicholas is out there?"

"Yeah, but it's not so much that as what she did to me."

Rachel crossed to the coffeepot and poured her some in a mug, then sat across from Jordan. "You're having a hard time forgiving her."

"Yes." She pushed her laptop to the side and cradled her coffee, the warmth from the drink doing nothing to take the chill from her fingers. "Everything would be so different if she hadn't kept my calls from Zachary."

"If you can't forgive her, how can you expect Zachary to forgive you?" Rachel sipped her drink.

Her sister's question threw her off balance. She stared down at her mug, trying to come up with an appropriate answer. She opened her mouth to say something. The situation between her and Zachary's mother was different, wasn't it?

But it wasn't. *The Lord forgives us, but He expects us to forgive others in return. How can I not?*

"I know it won't be easy, but don't you think you should make the first move? Show Zachary you can forgive."

Jordan shook her head. "I don't know if I can."

"Just think on it. We can't expect to receive forgiveness if we can't forgive."

"How did you become so wise?"

"It's the duty of an older sister." Rachel took another swig of her coffee.

Jordan shut down her laptop, her sister's advice nibbling at her defenses. "I think I'll pick Nicholas up at the ranch before anatomy class. Maybe by then, I'll know if I can forgive her and what to say."

Rising, her sister hugged her then took her mug to the sink. "I know you'll do the right thing."

With her chin cupped in her hand, Jordan stared at a spot across the kitchen as Rachel left. *Lord, I don't have to ask You what You think I should do. I know, but I don't know if I can do it. Please give me the strength and words to forgive Zachary's mother.*

Later after Jordan called Zachary to let him know she would pick up Nicholas, she headed out to the ranch early, hoping to catch his mother at Becca's. She took Tucker. Her son's pet had been missing him and moping around. When she parked behind the Rutgerses' car with an Arizona license plate, she kept the car windows down enough for Tucker to poke his nose out. Then, climbing from the Camaro, she fortified herself with a deep, cleansing breath and mounted the steps to the porch.

Becca answered her knock. Moving to the side to allow Jordan inside, Zachary's sister welcomed her with a smile. "Nicholas is at the barn with Zachary."

"I'm here to see your mother."

Her grin vanishing, Becca glanced toward the kitchen. "She's in there doing her daily crossword puzzle. Should I referee?"

"No. Your mom and I need to come to an understanding."

"Agreed." Again Becca made another quick look toward the kitchen. "She was thrilled to meet Nicholas yesterday evening. They're planning on staying the whole week and hope to spend as much time with him as possible. Dad's down at the barn with him and Zachary."

Jordan slowed her steps the closer she came to the kitchen. She wasn't sure how to begin a conversation with Zachary's mom. When she entered, the older woman looked up. Her sixty-plus years carved deep lines into her face. Lines at the moment that stressed her ire.

"You're early. Nicholas is at the barn." Putting her pencil down on the newspaper, Mrs. Rutgers pinched her lips even tighter together.

The cold thread that ran through her voice chilled Jordan, but she was determined to have this meeting with Zachary's mother. Before she'd left home, she'd read several passages in her Bible on forgiveness, trying to shore up her fledgling resolve to do what was right in the eyes of the Lord. "I know he's at the barn. I came early to talk to you."

"Why?"

Jordan sank onto the chair across from Mrs. Rutgers. "Don't you think we should talk with all that has happened? We owe it to Nicholas and Zachary."

Her eyebrows beetling together, she stared down at the crossword puzzle. "I suppose so. You kept our grandson from us for ten years. That was so wrong." Her voice strengthened its forceful tone as she spoke.

"And it wasn't wrong that you kept my calls from Zachary? If you had told him, you would have known."

"Why didn't you tell me that day why you were calling?"

Her words hit her like icicles piercing her flesh. "I wanted Zachary to be the first to know. I owed him that."

"Something you didn't do. Did you?"

She sucked in a deep breath, the hammering tap of her heartbeat pulsating against her rib cage. "I thought I was. I didn't know you wouldn't pass the message on. After you went on and on about him being engaged and then he didn't call, I thought he didn't want to talk to me." Remembering the pain and conflict that assaulted her at that time brought tears to her eyes. She might forgive Mrs. Rutgers, but she didn't want to break down and cry in front of the woman.

"You should have known he would want to know about his child."

"There was a part of me so hurt by his rejection that I convinced myself he wouldn't want to know." When Mrs. Rutgers started to say something to that last statement, Jordan held up her hand. "But there was a part of me that knew he would and couldn't bring myself to tell him. I'm sorry for what happened here, and I hope we can get past this for Nicholas's sake." *And mine. I'm tired of past events dictating my future.*

Mrs. Rutgers snorted. "I'll be civil to you when my grandson is around, but that's all I can promise." Bending over the puzzle, she picked up the pencil and jotted down some letters in the squares.

Jordan stared at the top of her silver hair. Rising, she clutched the back of the chair. "I forgive you for not telling Zachary about my calls, for lying to me about him being engaged. That's what I came to tell you. I can understand you wanting to protect your son. That's how I feel about Nicholas. Good day." Her rehearsed apology rolled from her lips like tumbleweed on a deserted road.

She marched toward the front of the house, not stopping to say anything to Becca. Tears burned her eyes, and she needed to get outside before she cried. On the porch the late-September air cooled her heated cheeks. The scent of honeysuckle along the front of the house floated to Jordan, reminding her of Granny's favorite fragrance. Thinking of her grandmother's parting words from Ephesians calmed her nerves. *And be ye kind one to another, tenderhearted, forgiving one another, even as God for Christ's sake hath forgiven you.*

She'd done what she'd come to do, and now she would

pick up Nicholas and take him to his anatomy class. Peace settled in her heart as she headed to her car and drove toward the barn.

Nicholas stood on a fence slat, leaning against the top rail. He watched Zachary in the corral getting ready to mount a chestnut horse with Mr. Rutgers holding the animal by the halter. Jordan parked next to Zachary's black truck and approached her son.

Nicholas peered at her, saw Tucker following her and hopped down. He stooped to pet his dog. Its tail wagged against his leg. "Dad's riding this horse for the first time. He's been working with the gelding getting him used to him being around the saddle, but he's still a bit skittish."

Jordan peered at Zachary in the ring. He talked to the animal in a soft, soothing tone as he held the reins in his left hand tightly. After putting his foot in the stirrup, he swung up onto the gelding's back in one fluid motion, putting his weight in the center of the horse's back. His father had backed off toward the fence where she and Nicholas stood on the other side while Zachary continued to murmur to the animal. The gelding pranced back for a few steps then settled down.

Tucker barked. Zachary glanced toward them, zeroing in on Jordan. For a few seconds their gazes locked.

Suddenly the dog slipped from Nicholas's grasp and darted into the corral, yelping. He crossed the paddock, heading near the gelding and Zachary in his pursuit of a cat that raced from the barn toward a large oak shading part of the paddock.

The horse jumped and sidestepped, then began bucking. In a split second, Zachary flew off the animal's back and landed with a thud on the dirt ground a few feet from the gelding. Jordan gasped. Tucker yapped at the bottom of the tree where the cat had disappeared. The loud sound echoed through the yard. The horse reared up and his hooves came down toward Zachary. He rolled, but one hoof clipped him on the leg.

Nicholas started to climb through the slats to get to his father while Nicholas's grandfather hurried out to the middle.

"Stay put," she said to her son and rushed to the gate into the corral. "Don't come in here. Get Tucker. Calm him down."

With her heart pounding, she dashed to Zachary while his father approached the horse cautiously. "Are you all right?"

"Yeah," he said, pain etched into his tanned features. "Don't, Dad. I'll take care of it. Leave him to me." Zachary rubbed the calf of his leg then struggled to stand.

Jordan put her arm around his middle to help him. He allowed her to for a second, then shrugged from her.

"Keep Nicholas out. You get out. And keep Tucker quiet." He hobbled toward the frightened gelding.

Jordan moved to the gate, but her attention focused fully on the scene in the corral. The horse's nostrils widened, pupils dilated. Out of the corner of her eye Jordan noticed Nicholas scoop Tucker up into his arms and quickly walk away from the oak. Blissful quiet reigned again except for the horse's snorts.

With his arms out in front of him, his hands up, palms outward, Zachary slowed his steps, saying, "Easy. Everything's okay. Easy. No one is gonna hurt you."

Jordan pictured again that time Zachary had fallen off the horse in the rodeo and broken his arm. It could have happened today, or if she hadn't been here, Nicholas could have been out in the middle of the corral before his father noticed. The gelding could have charged....

Don't go there. It didn't happen. Lord, how do I turn

*control over to You and stop getting so worked up over
anything out of my control?*

She splayed her hand over her chest as she inhaled then
exhaled.

Finally Zachary led the gelding toward the gate. Jordan
backed away with Nicholas plastered against her side. Her
gaze never left the horse as Zachary limped toward the
barn with his dad next to him.

"Did you see Dad? Nothing scares him."

These past six weeks she'd felt as though she'd had no
say in what was going on around her. She wasn't even
sure her homeschooling with Nicholas was working out.
Was she doing it right? What if her son lost ground in his
education because of her?

Nicholas started forward.

"Where are you going?"

"To make sure Dad's okay."

"First let's put Tucker in the car. We don't want any more
problems."

Nicholas slumped toward the Camaro and settled his
dog in the front seat. "He didn't mean to cause trouble."

"I know, hon. I shouldn't have let him out, but he was
so lonely for you." She strode toward the barn, keeping a
grasp on her son's shoulder.

Zachary released the gelding into a pasture with other
horses, and he immediately ran off. His father said something to Zachary, then hurried away, nodding to her and
Nicholas as he passed.

"I'm sorry about Tucker," Jordan said when she reached
Zachary.

"Bad timing. It happens. No problem." He took a step
and winced.

"You're hurt."

"I've been hurt worse before, and I doubt it will be the

last time. This is nothing. A cowboy is used to bumps and bruises."

Nicholas puffed out his chest. "Yeah, Mom. I fell off a horse and hurt my bottom. I was sore a few days, but it was no big deal."

"You fell off a horse?"

"Yeah. Didn't I tell you about it? It was last week. I was trying to open the gate to ride through it. I held on to it too long while Chief went on into the field."

"No, you two neglected to mention that."

Zachary compressed his lips, his nostrils flaring like the agitated gelding. "For this very reason. Nicholas is okay and learned a valuable lesson."

"It was one thing that it happened and an entirely different thing when I'm not kept informed."

Nicholas took his dad's hand. "I didn't want to worry you. You worry too much."

Father and son strolled toward the barn, leaving Jordan to stare at them. Her heart constricted at the thought she was losing her child. He might be her only one, because no matter how much she tried to move on after Zachary she hadn't been able to and now she knew the impossibility of that relationship.

She hurriedly followed the pair into the barn, catching Nicholas before he went into a stall. "We have to get going. You have a class today."

Her son's face brightened. "I almost forgot and I really want to hear what Dr. Reynolds has to say about the heart."

She wouldn't be half-surprised if Nicholas already knew most of what the doctor would impart to the students today. When he'd discovered what was wrong with him, he'd delved into everything he could get his hands on concerning his heart. If it had been too hard for him to read, she had read aloud for her son. It hadn't taken him long before she didn't have to.

Nicholas started for the double doors.

Zachary chuckled. "I once asked him to tell me about his heart defect, and it took all my willpower to keep my eyes from glazing over as he explained."

"Dr. Reynolds has been particularly patient with all Nicholas's questions during class."

"Do you stay?"

"No, I run errands, but I can tell by what he and Nicholas have said that he asks a lot of questions."

Nicholas placed his hand on his hip. "Mom, we're going to be late."

"At least I feel good about his math and science. The rest of the subjects I'm not so sure about." She strode away before Zachary had a chance to ask what she meant. She shouldn't have confessed her doubts about homeschooling Nicholas. Doubts she had to work through.

"How was class today? Did you learn anything more about the heart?" Jordan asked as she picked up Nicholas at the doctor's office where he held the biweekly classes.

"Yeah, a couple of things. Class got me to thinking. I need to be studying the anatomy of the different animals to help prepare me to be a veterinarian. There'll be similarities but also differences between species. When I'm older, I can help out at a vet's office. What do you think?"

"You've got some time before that."

"Dad said he would introduce me to his vet. I hope I can start taking college courses by age fifteen. You can help me plan that. Now that I'm being homeschooled, I can go at my own rate. I don't have to hold back."

"You've been holding back?"

"Some. I didn't like the other kids making fun of what

I knew. I never felt like I could be myself around my classmates."

After pulling into the driveway at her childhood home, Jordan shifted toward her son and took in his serious expression. "Hon, it's okay if you're a kid and you have fun."

"I am. I love going to the ranch, helping Dad with the horses. One day I'll be able to do what he does."

"Fall off a horse? Didn't you already?"

"Dad's like a horse whisperer. I want that kind of connection. I've been working with Tucker on that."

College in five years? Her son had his whole life mapped out while she was still struggling with hers. "Oh, I almost forgot to tell you, I got you signed up for art lessons."

"Do you think a cowboy would draw?"

"Excuse me?"

"Maybe I should do photography or learn how to play the harmonica."

"I thought you liked to draw and wanted to learn more."

"That was last month. Do you know that Dad plays the fiddle?"

"A violin?"

"No, it's called a fiddle. He took it up when he was on the rodeo circuit. Some of the guys had an informal little band." Nicholas tapped the side of his chin. "Yep, I'm thinking the harmonica would complement a fiddle. I'll ask Dad."

Had her son been watching a lot of old Western movies or something like that? Before she could say another word, he pushed open the car door and raced for the porch. She felt as though a tornado had flattened her. Her child was changing into someone she didn't know. Becoming more like Zachary.

Her stomach knotted as she trudged toward the house. Scratch the drawing lessons. Where could she find someone to teach her son the harmonica? Maybe photography would be a better choice. It would be easier to find a class for that.

When she entered the foyer, she called out to Nicholas. He came to the top of the stairs and peered over the banister.

"We need to get to work. I'll be up there in a minute. This week's essay is an expository one."

Nicholas groaned.

"You'll need to pick a topic and explain in detail about a certain event or situation. No editorial comments. Facts and other people's views."

"Anything I wish?"

"Yes, if it fits the type of essay."

"Great!" He fled down the upstairs hallway, the sound of his pounding footsteps resonating through the house.

The words *great* and *writing* never went hand in hand with Nicholas. She strode into the den where Granny usually was at this time of day to let her know they were home—which obviously she'd already heard—and see if she was okay. Granny had had a headache earlier, and when she'd left for the ranch, her grandmother was lying down in her bedroom.

Five minutes later Jordan entered Nicholas's room and came to an abrupt halt. A video clip of Zachary on the back of a bull at a rodeo bombarded her. When she saw him tumble to the ground as the horn sounded, the next few seconds snatched her breath.

Chapter Twelve

Nicholas glanced back at Jordan, then quickly clicked off the video.

She held up a trembling hand and pointed at the computer. "Where did you get that?"

"I found it online. I have all the rodeo clips of Dad, at least the ones I could find."

The image of the bull trampling Zachary shook her as though she had been there and seen the horrific sight of his battered body lying in the dirt. "I don't want you watching that or any ones like it."

"My essay is going to be about the rodeo. I was doing research." Nicholas turned totally around in his desk chair and faced her.

She folded her arms across her chest. She couldn't shake the picture from her mind. Zachary hurt. Not moving. "Find another topic."

"I know what happened to Dad that last time he rode. He told me about it. I'm not a baby. Quit trying to protect me."

Remain calm. Yes, she'd known an accident had caused Zachary's limp, but she'd never thought it had been as bad as what she'd seen. She waited half a minute to answer her son. "What do you suggest I do? Let you do whatever you want?"

He straightened his shoulders. "What are you afraid of? That I'll go out the first chance I get and ride a bull like Dad? I love riding horses, but I know I don't have what it takes to ride a bull. I don't want to learn. You can quit worrying about that. But I want to learn everything about something my father loves. He spent many years participating in the rodeo. A lot of the horses he raises end up in the rodeo. So what are you afraid of?"

A pressure in her chest expanded to encompass her whole body. She stared at her son and tried to come up with an answer to his question that didn't expose her fears. She couldn't. "I'm afraid of losing you." *I'm afraid I'll be alone.*

"To Dad?"

Tears lumping in her throat, she nodded. She'd centered her life around him for so long she didn't know what she would do if something happened to Nicholas. That one time waiting for him to come out of surgery had given her a glimpse of the fear that gripped her in a stranglehold. *How do I turn that over to You, Father?*

Nicholas leaped up, raced across the room and threw his arms around her. "You aren't going to lose me. I love you, but I love Dad, too. Can't I love both of you?"

She buried her face in his hair. "Yes. I haven't had to share you for ten years. Give me some time to get used to the idea."

"Sure." He leaned back, still clasping her. "But I want to learn about the rodeo. I already have a thesis statement."

The excitement in her son's voice wiped away her concerns. She'd never heard him so eager to write a paper. She had to trust in the Lord. "What happened to your father that last rodeo?"

"Have him tell you. I always believe in going to the primary source, so ask him."

"I will. I need to understand, too." She ruffled his hair. "So you've already got a thesis statement. This is a first."

Grinning from ear to ear, he moved back to the computer and brought up a blank screen. "Yes, but I want to do a lot more research. But the idea of a cowboy is disappearing and I think the rodeo is one of the last bastions of the cowboy ideal. Rugged. Fearless. Skilled."

Jordan swallowed several times. These thoughts hadn't just formulated in the past fifteen minutes. Nicholas had been thinking about it for a while. "Let me know when you're through with your research. We'll work on the rough draft together."

"I'd like to write the rough draft by myself first before we work together."

"Okay. I'll leave you to write."

Jordan left her son's bedroom and headed downstairs to the kitchen where she had her laptop. She would do her own online search of Zachary's name and see what video clips were posted. When she'd told Nicholas she needed to understand, she'd meant that. What had made Zachary get on the back of a two-thousand-pound bull? Take risks in his professional life but not his personal one?

"Mom, what are you doing here? I was coming up to Becca's in half an hour." Zachary moved out of the way to allow his mother into his house.

"I thought we would talk a few minutes before the barbecue. Before Nicholas and—" she tensed, her mouth firming in such a thin line her lips vanished.

"—Jordan arrive. I think it's about time we talk, too."

"You do? You've been avoiding me all week."

He rubbed his nape. "I know. I haven't figured out how I feel about anything. Everything has happened so fast these past weeks."

His mother strode into the living room and took a seat on the couch. "But we need to talk about what I did all those years ago. Avoiding the subject won't make it go away."

Restless energy surged through him. He remained standing. "Why didn't you tell me about Jordan's calls? I know you said you were protecting me...." His words trailed into the silence. Were his mother and Jordan alike—protecting their sons?

"Ever since she came to see me last Monday, I've—"

"Wait, you talked with Jordan on Monday?"

"Yeah, she came to tell me she'd forgiven me. Can you believe that? She forgives me while she's the one who kept the fact you had a son from us."

"She did," he murmured, sinking onto the chair nearby, the spike of energy suddenly siphoning from him.

"I told her how I felt."

"How?"

"I'm angry like you. We missed ten years of Nicholas's life. Ten!"

But I'm not angry anymore. That realization settled over him, calming his restless spirit. "She had her hands full with Nicholas's illness and raising him alone."

"That was her choice."

"True. But she was hurt when I didn't call. She thought I didn't want to have anything to do with her. You told her I was engaged when I wasn't."

"Are you defending her?" Anger sparked his mother's eyes and deepened the lines on her face.

"I'm trying to understand her. I'm trying to make this situation with Nicholas work."

"She did you wrong. Stay away from her."

Zachary bolted to his feet and paced. "I can't. I have to think about Nicholas now." Pausing, he rotated toward his mother. "Why didn't you tell me she called?"

"I told you I was protecting you. She hurt you bad. I still remember how you were after you two broke up. You needed to get on with your life without her."

The similarities hit him full force. So like Jordan with Nicholas. "I needed to know I was having a child." His hands balled at his sides. So many emotions swirled around inside him like a dust storm on the prairie.

"I did what any mother would do. Looking out for the best interests of her child, no matter what."

"Including lying?"

Her face pale, she stared down at her hands twining in her lap. "I wouldn't have kept anything like Nicholas from you if I had known." When she lifted her head, tears shone in her eyes. "I would have done it differently. Given you the messages. But she didn't tell me."

His mother's words cut through his heart like a piece of barbed wire. He had enough turmoil in his life without adding conflict with his mother to the list. "Let's just drop this. It's in the past. We can't change it now."

She rose. "I agree."

"But I need you to be civil to Jordan at the barbecue for Nicholas's sake."

"I'll do my best. But why does she have to come to a family dinner?"

"Because she's my child's mother. Becca and her have become friends. And Nicholas wants her there."

She tilted her head and pinned her gaze on him. "But not you?"

"I want her there for all those reasons." He evaded what his mother really wanted to know because he didn't have an answer. Ever since Jordan had returned to Tallgrass, his emotions had been bound in knots—ones he couldn't slip loose easily.

"I'm gonna miss Grandma and Granddad when they return to Arizona in a couple of days." Nicholas squirmed in the front seat of Jordan's Camaro the closer they got to the ranch.

"I'm glad you're enjoying their visit." But thinking about her talk with Zachary's mother made her tighten her hands about the steering wheel.

Jordan pulled into the gravel road that led to Becca's house. The closer she came, the more her stomach constricted and roiled. She wished she had her son's excitement about this barbecue.

When she parked in front, Nicholas leaped from the car, raced toward the porch and disappeared inside. The sound of voices, a laugh, floated to her. This was Nicholas's family. Not hers. She should have stayed home. And yet, she and Zachary needed to do things without Nicholas—get to know each other as adults. Maybe she should ask him to go on a picnic like they had as teenagers.

But first she had to get through the barbecue with his mother.

Dropping her head on the steering wheel, she closed her eyes and prayed for strength and patience to get through this afternoon. *I can do this.* Then she remembered Mrs. Rutgers's words and the chill that emanated from the woman when she'd talked with her in the kitchen the other day. The chill enveloped her as she sat in the front seat.

A rap on her window startled her. She twisted around. Zachary's handsome face filled her vision. The ice that encased her melted away.

He opened the door. "Are you okay?"

The concern in his voice soothed some of her tension. *I can do this for Nicholas.* She relaxed and smiled. "Just working myself up to see your mother again."

"Ah." He straightened. "She'll behave herself. She promised me."

"I wish you hadn't had to ask." She climbed from the car.

"Me, too. But I imagine you can understand her feelings since you're a mother."

Jordan started for the house, hoping the next few hours sped by in a blur. When she neared the porch, laughter wafted to her from inside. She slanted a look toward Zachary next to her. "Does Becca need help in the kitchen?"

He chuckled. "A strategic escape. Not bad. I'm sure she would enjoy your company."

When she entered, she said hi to everyone then made her way toward the kitchen. At the door she peered back at Zachary's mom, who nailed her with a sharp gaze. What was the woman thinking? She shouldn't have accepted the invitation.

"I'm so glad you came, Jordan." With her hands full, Becca shut the refrigerator with a push of her hip. "I could use you to put the potato salad together. The potatoes are cooked, but that's as far as I've gotten."

"I'd be glad to."

"It'll beat playing soccer." Becca gave her a knife and cutting board.

"Soccer?"

"Yeah, Zachary and Paul thought it be would a great idea to have an impromptu game. Of course, they didn't take into account I don't play and neither does Mom. I hurried in here to finish making the dinner and left them to pick teams."

"So your mom is going to join us?"

Chuckling, Becca shook her head. "Dad and Mom are gonna be cheerleaders."

"Nicholas doesn't know how to play." Jordan began dicing the potatoes.

"My youngest doesn't, either. Nicholas will learn. Zachary is a great teacher."

"Speaking of teaching, how do you homeschool three children? I feel like I'm in over my head half the time. I've been doing it a month, and I don't know if I'm doing it the right way."

"There's no one right way. What you do will depend on your child and how he learns. In Nicholas's case, he loves to learn. A lot of what he does will be self-directed whereas with Mike I have to be on top of him every step of the way. For Nicholas, you'll have to make sure he covers all he needs and doesn't get stuck on one subject. I know he's great with math, and from what Zachary has said, he doesn't like to write. You'll have to make sure he does it."

Jordan took the boiled eggs and began chopping them to add to the large mixing bowl. "Yeah, I've been doing that. He whines when I make him write, even using the computer. With everything else he doesn't give me any problems."

"When it doesn't come easy or they don't like it, they balk at doing it. You should see Ashley with math. She hates it. There are times I've lost my patience with her, and I don't like doing that. Frustrating." Taking a wooden spoon, Becca stirred the brownie mixture.

"I know what you mean. He's so smart, but he gets frustrated with himself when he starts putting his thoughts down on paper." After adding the pickled relish, Jordan sliced a red onion. "Except with this newest writing project. He's really gotten into it."

"What's it about?"

"An expository essay about the rodeo. He told me he was almost through with the rough draft. I've seen some of it. It's the best writing he's ever done."

"That's my brother's influence."

Jordan cocked her head, thinking back over the past weeks and the changes she'd seen in Nicholas. "Yes, it is. Until Zachary, I didn't realize how much my son needed a father. It's always been just the two of us and that has seemed fine. But it wasn't really."

After pouring the chocolate batter into an oblong pan, Becca stuck it into the oven. "Kids do best when they have a stable environment with two loving parents."

Jordan paused in cutting up the onion, her eyes watering from its strong odor. If only she had swallowed her pride and hurt years ago, Nicholas could have had that kind of environment. *Lord, I've been so wrong. How do I fix this?*

"You okay?"

She brushed her hand across her wet cheek. "It's the onion." *It's me. I messed up.*

The chatter from the living room died down. The bang of the front door—more than once—echoed through the house.

"I guess they decided on their teams. Want to go be a cheerleader?" Becca laid the dish rag she'd used to clean the counter into the sink.

After scraping the onion pieces into the bowl, Jordan started on the celery. "I'm almost finished. You go ahead. If we arrive together, they'll want us to be on a team."

"Yeah, you're probably right, except I doubt any of them would want me." Becca patted her stomach. "I've really got to start exercising." Before she left, she added, "Jordan, you're doing fine. A lot of homeschooling moms ask the questions you are. Am I providing the best education? Am I missing anything? As you've been discovering, the Helping Hands Homeschooling group is a great place to get support and help. You aren't alone in doing this."

Jordan sighed as Becca strolled from the kitchen toward the front of the house. She felt confident in her work as a graphic design artist and even felt good about the job she'd done raising Nicholas to be a responsible young man. But she still wrestled with what was best educationally for her son. It was a comfort to know that other parents went through the same dilemma.

After putting all the ingredients for the potato salad in the bowl, Jordan stirred them together then put the dish into the refrigerator. The scent of chocolate permeated the air and made her stomach gurgle with hunger. She took a few moments to clean up, trying to delay going outside as long as possible, but when Zachary appeared in the entrance, she knew she couldn't any longer.

"I came in to make sure you hadn't gotten lost finding your way outside." He rested his shoulder against the door frame.

"No," she said with a laugh. "I'll be there in a few minutes."

"We kinda need you now."

"Why?" She turned to face him fully, the mischievous sparkle in his eyes accelerating her heartbeat.

"Paul talked Becca into playing. We need another player to even out the teams. Mom and Dad are even participating."

Placing her hand on her hip, she gave him a pout. "You know how I am when it comes to sports."

"I know how you used to be. I'm not sure now." The gleam in his expression brightened.

"Well, let me reassure you, I'm lousy at anything having

to do with a ball. And if I'm not mistaken soccer has one."

Zachary closed the distance between them and grabbed her hand. "Come on. It's about time you got over your fear of being hit with a ball."

"Hey, I've been hit with one and let me tell you it hurts." As he urged her toward the front door, she tried to frown, but her mouth refused to cooperate. "How in the world did Paul talk Becca into playing?"

"I'm not one hundred percent positive, but I think it was something about if my mother could do it, she could, too."

As Zachary dragged her laughing out of the house, Jordan decided playing a game of soccer could be fun—that was until she saw Zachary's mother. Her scowl darkened her eyes, and the older woman turned away. Jordan didn't know what would be worse, being on the same team as Mrs. Rutgers or the opposite one.

Later that day, the scent of hamburgers grilling saturated the fall air. A crisp breeze cooled the evening. A door shutting drew Zachary around. Jordan crossed the yard with a large platter.

"Becca said to put the burgers on this when they're done." She placed it on a table near the barbecue grill and turned to leave.

He didn't want her to go. He hadn't talked to her much since the soccer game earlier. "Stay. Keep me company. You've been awfully quiet. That's not like you."

"It's been a bit awkward."

"Because of Mom?"

"You are perceptive."

"Ouch. I think I hear a touch of sarcasm." He began

flipping over the thick patties. "Mom hasn't said anything to you."

"No. But…" She snapped her mouth closed and averted her gaze.

"But what?"

"It's obvious I'm not wanted here and that makes it uncomfortable. If we'd been playing football, I think she would have tackled me, and I was on her team."

"Give her time."

"You aren't the least bit angry at her for not telling you I called?"

Zachary set the spatula on the platter and faced Jordan. "I'm not happy it happened, but she thought she was doing what was best for me."

She started to say something, shook her head and turned away. Walking to the edge of the patio, she stared at the horses in the pasture behind Becca's house. A strong urge to hold her and take away the hurt he'd seen flash into her eyes overwhelmed him. He stiffened, resisting Jordan's lure.

When she spun around, a neutral expression descended over her features. "Are you still mad at me?"

Was he? "No, not really. For Nicholas's sake, I let go of my anger. It doesn't do any good now, and like we talked about before, we need to be a team for our son."

"Then I have a proposition for you. I think we should spend some time together alone getting to know each other better to see if we can find a common ground."

"You want us to date?" The idea should have sent him into a panic. Surprisingly it made sense.

"No. Just two people getting to know each other better. For Nicholas's sake."

"Sure. Do you have something in mind?"

"As a matter of fact, I do. How about next Friday afternoon? We'll have a picnic lunch. My treat."

"Hey, Zachary, the burgers are smoking," Becca yelled from the back door stoop.

He whirled around, snatched up the spatula and scooped up the patties before they became charred. Jordan had always had the ability of taking his mind off what he should be doing. What in the world had he agreed to?

"I want everything to be perfect today." Jordan finished packing the picnic basket with a container of peach cobbler on Friday.

"Child, you're gonna need a forklift to pick that thing up." Granny waved her hand toward the wicker basket.

"Didn't you tell me the way to a man's heart was through his stomach?"

"That I did. That's how I got your grandpa. Now with Doug, he cooks as good as I do. It's kinda nice having a man cook for me. In fact, we've got a date tonight."

"You two are getting mighty serious."

"We don't have the luxury of a long-drawn-out courtship. Time is a-ticking." Granny snapped her fingers several times as she spoke. "Remember that, child. You don't have the luxury, either. You and your young man have been apart long enough. Nicholas needs a whole family."

"I'm thinking about it."

"So where are you going today?"

"To Miller Falls."

"Ah, good thinking. Very romantic."

That was what she was counting on. Miller Falls was one of the places they had gone to as teenagers. It held special memories for her, and she hoped for Zachary, too. If there was to be anything between them, maybe they would discover it there.

The doorbell chimed. Jordan hefted the basket from the table, leaned down and kissed Granny on the cheek then started toward the foyer. "Have a great time with Doug."

Granny chuckled. "I will. And when I get back this evening, I want to hear all about your date."

At the entrance into the kitchen Jordan glanced at her grandmother. "Shh. Don't say that. It's not a date."

"Keep telling yourself that and maybe you'll really believe it."

By the time she reached the foyer, Nicholas had opened the door and let Zachary inside. "Are we going to practice tomorrow during our riding lesson for HHH Junior Rodeo?"

"Yep. We have only a week to go." Zachary tousled his son's hair.

Jordan set the heavy basket on the tile floor. "Don't forget your assignment for anatomy class. Aunt Rachel will be taking you this afternoon."

"I've already done it." He swung back to Zachary. "Dad, don't leave yet. I've got something for you." He raced up the stairs.

"Do you know what?" Zachary asked.

"You've never been good about surprises."

"You aren't, either."

"I've got a pretty good idea, but I'm not telling."

He frowned but didn't put much into the expression. "Is where we're going a surprise?"

She gestured toward the basket at her feet. "We're going on a picnic."

"Where?"

"Sorry. My lips are sealed."

Nicholas hurried down the stairs with a manila envelope in his hand. When he gave it to Zachary, her son thrust his shoulders back and lifted his chin. "I wrote this."

Zachary started to open the envelope.

"No, read it later." A blush stained her child's cheeks.

"Okay," Zachary said slowly, glancing between them. "Are you ready?"

She nodded.

He picked up the basket and stepped out onto the porch.

When she joined him outside, she stopped him with a hand on his arm. "I'm driving."

"Are you going to blindfold me, too?"

"What a great idea! Then where we're going will really be a surprise. Let me go back inside—" she pivoted toward the front door "—and get a scarf to use."

"By the time you get back out here, I'll be halfway down the street heading home."

With both hands on her hips, she faced him. "You aren't playing fair."

"I really don't like surprises."

"Okay, no blindfold, but I'm still driving."

"Then you'll have to use my truck. It's parked behind yours in the driveway." He descended the porch steps and tied down the basket in the back of his pickup.

When Jordan approached the driver's door, he tossed her the keys and rounded the front to slide into the passenger's seat. She backed out onto the street and headed toward the highway outside of town.

"You're the first person I've let drive my truck."

"I am?" She glanced at his white-knuckled grip on the handhold above the side window.

"Yep, and I still have two years of payments left on it."

She laughed. "Are you, in your not-so-subtle way, telling me I better not have a wreck?"

"Yes, ma'am."

"Then why did you let me drive?" The idea he had warmed her.

"I thought it was time."

At a stop sign, she fixed her attention fully on Zachary. "Time for what?"

"To give you a little trust."

"With your truck?"

"With my life."

Their gazes locked together. Jordan couldn't look away. Her throat contracted, and suddenly she wished they were anywhere but on a road waiting to pull out onto the highway. A blare of a horn behind her startled her. She dragged her attention away from Zachary and faced forward.

"To reassure you, I haven't had a wreck or a ticket. I'm a very good driver, but if I remember correctly when we were going together, you had one wreck and two tickets for speeding."

"But not in years. I'm a changed man."

Yes, he was different. More serious. Reserved. And when she caught a certain glimpse of Zachary when he wasn't looking, she saw a hint of tragedy in his eyes. Was she the one who had put it there? Or was it someone or something else?

After traveling five minutes north on the highway, Zachary said, "I know where we going. The south end of Prairie Lake."

"Nope."

She continued past the entrance to the park he mentioned. Another ten minutes and she turned down a narrow two-lane road.

"Miller Falls," Zachary murmured almost as if to himself.

"Yep. I thought it would be nice to visit somewhere we

had good times at. We didn't just date. We were friends. I want us to capture that again."

"Is that the truth?"

The skepticism in his question hurt. "Yes. Part of the reason we broke up eleven years ago was because we stopped communicating with each other. We both got wrapped up in our own world and forgot the other's. You spent that last summer going to rodeos, and I went to the Sooner Art Institute for a month."

"I remember. We saw each other in passing until the middle of August. I was trying to make some money to help us get started."

"I know but every time you rode in the ring I could hardly breathe until you were finished. There were times I wouldn't even watch. As you got more and more involved in bull riding, I got more scared."

"Why didn't you say anything to me?"

Jordan pulled into a small gravel parking lot not far from the creek and waterfall. Angling toward Zachary, she looked right at him. "Because you loved doing it. I didn't want to be the one to take that away from you. I thought if I got away and could get some perspective on our situation it would be okay."

"Then we fought and broke up."

"You didn't understand my art and I didn't understand your need to participate in rodeos. I didn't like football, but I would have preferred you taking that football scholarship offered to you."

One corner of his mouth lifted. "Don't tell anyone around here, but I didn't care that much about playing football. I certainly didn't want to in college."

"No, your heart was somewhere else. So why didn't you just go on the rodeo circuit rather than join the army?"

He stared out the windshield, his mouth lashing into

a tight-lipped grimace. "I was a fool. I started going out with the guys, partying. Anything to forget you. Two of us enlisted after drinking. I thought if I could see the world some, get away from Oklahoma and all the memories, even the rodeo, that everything would be all right. When I realized my mistake thinking that, it was too late. I was in basic training. I haven't drank since then."

"How many years were you in the army?"

"Four. I got some training, I saw the world and I went to school." He opened the door, hopped to the ground and reached back to get the basket.

She knew after he'd left the army that he'd become a professional bull rider for five years and was world champion for three straight years before his accident. Although she couldn't bring herself to watch that video again, she did watch others where he'd ridden to victory. Seeing him talk after getting his first world championship helped her to understand a little of the lure of what he did. His face had shown excitement and a sense of accomplishing something important, the same expression she'd seen when he had finished his ride and left the ring.

He came around and opened her door. "Ready?"

She climbed down and pocketed his keys. "I wish it was warmer. We could have gone swimming like that one time."

"This would be a fun place to bring Nicholas, especially next summer."

"Once he learns to swim."

Halting, Zachary rotated toward her, both eyebrows raised. "He doesn't know how to swim?"

She shook her head. "He was sick for a long time. We didn't have access to a pool in South Carolina. I lived in a little house, but there was no neighborhood pool."

He started forward. "Well, that's gonna change. He

might not always swim in a pool here, but places like this are great in the summer."

"Up until a couple of years ago, he didn't have the energy or desire. Now Nicholas is wanting to do all he's been missing."

"Like learning to ride?"

"Yep. That was top on his list when we moved here."

Looking back seven weeks, she wondered if her sister had told her the ranch she was sending her to was owned by Zachary if she would have come that day. Probably not. Actually, definitely not. But now she saw where the Lord was leading her. She needed to make amends to Zachary and bring them together as a family—at least Nicholas and his father, if not her, too. This outing renewed her hope it was possible.

"There's still so much I want to know about Nicholas." Zachary set the basket down on the ground under a large oak tree near the waterfall.

The sound of its water pouring over the rocks above and crashing down into the pool echoed through the small glade and faded into the woods that surrounded the place. Sunlight dappled the glittering surface like sparkling diamonds strewn across a pale blue carpet. The scent of pine and earth hung in the air.

Jordan opened the basket and withdrew the blanket. As she spread it under the oak, she gestured toward the manila envelope. "I suggest you read his essay as a start."

Stretching out on the blanket, he withdrew the papers and began reading. Intense concentration creased his forehead. Then slowly his expression went from surprise to awe.

When he finished, he peered at her sitting next to him. "He thinks the cowboy is the epitome of what this country stands for. He even draws parallels between the jousting of knights in medieval times to the contestants in a rodeo, competing for the prize. A lot of thought went into this."

"It's a tribute to you. He watched hours of videotape, mostly of you, before he wrote this. I didn't help him hardly at all, which is most unusual when he writes."

Zachary swallowed hard. "I didn't know he was doing this. He asked me some questions this past week about what I did, how I felt, but I just thought it was his curiosity."

"He wanted to understand what drove you to risk your life each time you got on the back of a bull."

"He obviously listens well."

"Until I read this last night, I didn't have a clue why you did it."

"'The thrill and adrenaline rush is unbelievable, but what really got me back on a two-thousand-pound, bucking bull each time was the faith of totally putting myself in God's hands' was the answer three-time world champion Zachary Rutgers stated when asked why he was a bull rider." Zachary lifted his gaze from the essay to look into her eyes. "That was my answer word for word and he didn't even write it down. Amazing."

She smiled. "Yes, Nicholas is amazing."

"Tell me about his heart defect, his surgery. I know you've told me some, but that had to be such a difficult time for both of you. I need to understand like you and Nicholas did about my bull riding."

"When he started school, Nicholas caught everything. He was always sick—small for his age. Finally our family physician diagnosed Nicholas with atrial septal defect. Usually it's repaired with a catheter. Nicholas got one, but then it became infected. He almost died. He was put on long-term antibiotics, lots of blood work, doctors. The catheter had to be removed and repaired surgically. All of this took a toll on Nicholas."

"And not you?"

Thinking back to that time brought a rush of memories of the hospital, long hours of doubt if Nicholas would be all right, sleepless nights, worry, prayers, tears. Her stomach still clenched anytime she visited someone in a hospital and got a whiff of that antiseptic scent. "Once Nicholas started recovering, I was fine."

Zachary clasped her palm. "You were? You're still scared for him and try to protect him."

She yanked her hand away. "What you really mean is that I'm overprotective."

He indicated an inch with his forefinger and thumb. "Maybe a little. The doctor said he is fine now. As I've said, a boy has to have breathing room."

"And guidance."

"Are you ready for him to compete in the HHH Junior Rodeo competition?"

"Barrel racing?"

"Yes, that's one thing."

"Do you really think he's ready?"

"I was doing what he's doing at six."

"And look what happened to you." She pulled her legs up and clasped them to her chest.

He lifted his shoulders in a shrug. "I survived, and I'm now doing something else I wanted to do—raising horses." Rubbing his hands together, he grinned. "I don't know about you, but I'm starving. What do we have for lunch?"

"A couple of your favorites. Or at least they used to be." Jordan scooted toward the basket and dug inside, bringing the first container out. "Fried chicken, extra crispy. Then I have a cucumber-tomato salad as well as a pasta one, slices of homemade bread and butter and for dessert peach cobbler."

Zachary peeked beneath the foil at the chicken and picked up several pieces. "Don't tell Nicholas how much I love this."

"Oh, he knows. He helped me with this lunch."

"I still can't believe I have a son who is a vegetarian."

"He isn't your usual child."

"I'm discovering that every time I'm with him." He finished loading his paper plate with the various dishes.

After she selected what she wanted to eat, she bowed her head and blessed the food. "Dig in. What you don't eat you can take home with you if you want."

Several bites later, he looked straight at her and said, "A guy sure could get used to food like this. This is delicious."

"You can thank Granny for teaching me how to cook."

"I'll do that. Your grandmother is quite a character. How are she and Doug getting along?" He took a sip of his bottled water.

"According to my mother, too well. She thinks Granny is too old to carry on like a twenty-year-old."

"Your mom doesn't want to see your grandmother with a man?"

"I think she's jealous. She's been divorced for more than twenty years and has dated off and on over the years, but she never has found anyone who interested her. Lately she has declared she isn't going to date anymore. She loves her life like it is."

"And you don't believe her?"

"Nope and neither does Rachel. My sister has even tried to fix her up with a couple of older men who were friends of her husband's. It didn't work out. Rachel has decided matchmaking isn't for her."

"Contrary to a certain grandmother and young boy."

Again Zachary's gaze snagged hers from across the blanket and held her linked to him. She swallowed her bite of salad past the lump in her throat. The intensity in his eyes heated her cheeks. For a moment she felt as though she were the most important person in his life. The warmth from her blush spread through her body.

"They don't seem to be too bad lately," she murmured, wetting her dry lips.

"Maybe they've given up on us."

"Maybe." Was there any hope for them? Had Nicholas and Granny realized there wasn't? "But I have to warn you, usually Nicholas is relentless and determined when he is after something. It's those qualities that helped him through his illness. He rarely cried when he was hurting. He was so brave." Tears sprang into her eyes when she thought back over that time, the pain he was going through evident on his face even though he tried to mask it. She closed her eyes, a wet drop dripping out and coursing down her face.

Zachary leaned close, wiped his thumb across her cheek, then cupped the back of her neck to draw her nearer. "You aren't by yourself with Nicholas anymore. I'm here to help."

His murmured words spoken into her hair as he hugged her against his chest made her almost believe there was a chance for her and Zachary. Then she remembered the invisible barrier always in place even when he held her close. As though he kept a small part of himself from her and that no matter what she did that wouldn't change.

With his thumb under her chin, he raised it so she stared into his eyes. "You've done a great job with Nicholas."

The compliment washed over her. She snuggled closer, wanting so much more than Zachary was willing to share. And it was her fault the situation was like that.

"If I could change what happened eleven—"

He settled his mouth over hers, stealing the rest of her sentence. For that brief moment when his lips connected with hers, all her doubts fled. Only possibilities lay ahead. Her heartbeat kicked up a notch, matching the faster tempo of his that she felt against his chest.

When he moved back, framing her face in his hands, his dazed expression vanished to be replaced with uncertainty, his eyebrows slashing downward, his gaze narrowing. "I shouldn't have done that. It only complicates things."

He surged to his feet and stuck his hands into his front pockets. "I'm sorry. That won't happen again." Striding away, he headed for the pool and stood on its edge, staring at the waterfall.

Jordan curled her legs up against her body, hugging them to her and laying her forehead on her knees. She'd crashed from a high plateau into a bottomless pit. Just as she thought she might be breaking down the barrier between them, Zachary pulled back and erected the wall even higher.

Chapter Thirteen

What had he been thinking? Kissing Jordan like that? Zachary plowed his hand through his hair, trying to bring order to his reeling thoughts. Today as she'd talked about Nicholas being in the hospital and having surgery, all he could think about was he should have been there. Then he saw her tears and all common sense evaporated.

As he listened to the creek plunging into the pool from above, the sound calmed him enough to turn back toward Jordan and cover the space between them. She'd put away the food except the peach cobbler and had a sketch pad out. Her head bent over the sheet, he couldn't see what she was drawing until she peered up at him. A shadow darkened her eyes and constricted his gut.

Lord, how do I maintain my distance from her and stay on friendly terms for Nicholas's sake? I'm not doing a good job of it. I've hurt her. And I don't like that.

"I shouldn't have kissed you." He eased down on the blanket at the other end from her.

"Then why did you?"

He waved his arm around the glade. "This place. Isn't

that why you brought me here? To have me remember how it once was between us?"

She stared at her sketch pad with the beginnings of a portrait of him. "Yes," she whispered, a raw edge to the word. When she reestablished visual contact with him, the shadow was gone. "But you don't need to worry about me doing anything like this again."

"I owe you an explanation."

"Isn't it obvious you can't forgive me?"

He ignored her question and said instead, "I never told you everything about my accident that ended my career as a bull rider."

"I saw it on the video. Nicholas showed it to me."

He sucked in a ragged breath. "I've never brought myself to watch it, but it's out there on the Internet for the whole world to see." A sharp pain, as if he felt the hooves of the bull all over again, pierced him. "Like Nicholas I suffered from an infection. The trampling caused mine. I've been left with a limp, twinges that remind me of the accident, especially when the weather changes, and I can't have kids. Nicholas will be my only child."

"No children?"

"The scar tissue was extensive." He severed eye contact with her. "When my fiancée found out the extent of my injury, she hightailed it out of my life."

"I'm sorry, Zachary."

"You should have more kids. You're a good mother. I know you've always wanted more than one."

"That's why you pulled away?"

"Part of the reason. Our time together as a couple is over. Has been for years." *Don't pursue this. You need more than I can offer.* He flicked his hand toward the pad. "I see you're still drawing."

She peered at him for a long moment as though deciding

whether to continue the conversation or not. "I don't do it as much as I used to. I'm trying to get back into it again."

He released a breath he didn't even realize he was holding until she dropped the subject of why they weren't suited together. "I'm glad. You were always so good. Can I see that?"

She flipped the lid over the drawing. "I'm not through. I'll show you when I am. How about some peach cobbler?"

"You know I'll never pass up one of your desserts." As she dished up his portion, he added, "Nicholas has been wanting me to take him to a rodeo. There's one next Friday in Bartlesville. I'd like to take him then. It'll be our guys' night out."

Her mouth tightened. "Sure."

"I promise I won't try and get him to pursue anything having to do with the rodeo."

"Next weekend will be a big one with the rodeo on Friday and HHH Junior Rodeo on Saturday."

He took a bite of the cobbler, the dessert melting in his mouth with just the right sweetness. "Mmm. This is great." After another scoop of it, he said, "I'll have Nicholas spend the night Friday and he can help me the next morning get ready for HHH Junior Rodeo."

"I'll be there early. I signed up to help set up the activities."

"Then come early and have breakfast with Nicholas and me. I'm sure he'll want to tell you all about the rodeo."

"Is that your roundabout way of asking me to fix breakfast for you two?"

"No, if you don't mind having cold cereal." He really did need to learn to cook now that he had a child part of the time. He still had a long way to go to be the father he wanted to be. He hated playing catch-up, especially with something so important as his son.

* * *

Jordan parked in front of Zachary's house early Saturday morning, just hours before the ranch would be crowded with families from the Helping Hands Homeschooling group participating in the HHH Junior Rodeo. Sitting and staring at the front porch, she couldn't bring herself to move from the car. When Zachary had picked Nicholas up yesterday afternoon to attend the rodeo, she'd wanted to go with them. She'd almost said something to them as they left. But then Zachary's words about it being their guys' night out stopped her. She swallowed the request, a heaviness in the pit of her stomach.

She was elated that her son and his father were bonding, spending time doing special activities. But she couldn't help feeling left out. The times all three of them had spent together made her want even more a complete family—a mother, father and child. Children, actually.

Zachary, though, couldn't have any more kids. His revelation had stunned her, but did it make any difference in the long run? Did it change her feelings about him? No, she wasn't like his ex-fiancée. She loved him no matter what, but at the waterfalls, he'd hammered home where they stood. Friends only—and then that only because of Nicholas.

His silence when she'd asked him if he'd forgiven her had been her answer. He couldn't get past what had happened eleven years ago. When he looked at her, he still saw her betrayal—like his fiancée's. Nothing she did would change that. It really wasn't because she deserved to have more children. Nothing he said really made her feel any differently.

He might as well have shouted it from the cliff surrounding the pool. She and Zachary would share Nicholas like a divorced couple. She had to move on.

Would her son begin to prefer his father's company to hers? Would she lose her child to Zachary? She hated thinking like that, but suddenly she felt in a competition for Nicholas's love.

The front door flew open, and her son ran out of the house, a grin plastered all over his face. By the time he'd reached the car, Jordan stood and grabbed the bag of groceries for breakfast.

"You're up early. Did you sleep any last night?" she asked Nicholas, who hugged her. She closed her eyes and relished the feel of his arms around her. How long would this last?

He walked next to her toward the house. "Nope. Too excited. Especially after seeing what real cowboys do."

"So you enjoyed seeing your first rodeo?'

"Yep." He hooked his thumbs into his jeans pockets. "One day I'm going to be as good at roping as Dad."

"Where is your dad?"

"He's trying to fix breakfast."

"He is? I thought I would cook for you two."

"He muttered something about having to learn. He called Aunt Becca and got some instructions, but I don't think he has the hang of it."

"Why?"

"You'll see." He tugged her toward the entrance.

The second she stepped into the house she knew why her son had said that. A burning smell drifted from the kitchen. "What's he making?"

"Pancakes. He used a box mix, but it isn't working very well."

"You think?" she said with a laugh and headed toward the back.

When she entered the kitchen, gray smoke poured from the skillet on the stove. On the counter sat a cookie sheet with burnt toast on it. Zachary snatched the frying pan off the burner and dumped its contents into the sink then turned the cold water on. A sizzling sound filled the silence, and steam bellowed from the skillet.

He whirled around. When he saw her, relief flooded his features. "I pulled the toast out of the oven and buttered the other side, then stuck it back in. That's when the pancakes I put on were getting a little too brown, so I flipped them. Thankfully they still looked edible. But everything after that went downhill. I was pouring the juice when I smelled the toast burning. Just as I took the pan out, the pancakes..." He waved his hand toward the sink. "All I want to know is how in the world do you coordinate putting a meal on the table with everything done at the right time?"

"Practice." She tried to contain her smile but couldn't.

"Yeah, like roping, Dad."

"So I get to look forward to more of these types of disasters?"

"Maybe you should take it in stages. One dish at a time."

He blew out a breath. "We'd starve at that rate."

"I'll clean this up and make some omelets. You can fix the toast while I do that." She opened the oven. "For starters you need to lower the rack so it's not so near the broiler." Taking the oven mitts, she adjusted it for Zachary. "That should help it not brown so quickly." She spun around. "Or better yet, buy a toaster. Much easier. You put it on a setting and leave the work to it."

"Can I help?" Nicholas asked.

"You can set the table." Jordan withdrew a mug from the cabinet, poured some coffee and took a sip. "Not too bad."

"I did something right."

Zachary's smile renewed the dreams she had about being a family. She quickly shoved them away. She needed to protect herself from getting hurt any more than she already was. *Friends only.*

Jordan sat across from Zachary later that afternoon at a picnic table under a pecan tree. All the races and competition had been completed half an hour ago, and Nicholas had come in third in the barrel race. In his roping demonstration he'd managed to land his lasso around the sawhorse twice as he rode by it. When her son competed in the sheep race, she'd laughed so hard her sides had hurt. Nicholas didn't have one problem in his events and the grin on his face had made it all worth it.

Lifting a bottle, she took a swig of water. A sigh escaped her lips as she relaxed for the first time in hours. "It's a good thing we only do this once a year. It's a lot of work putting this on."

Becca joined her and Zachary, sliding in next to her brother on the bench. "I heard Nancy and some of the others talking about doing this in the spring and fall. Everyone has had so much fun."

Zachary groaned.

"I'll do more next time. And Paul," Becca quickly said. "The ranch is a perfect place for it."

"I don't know about that. It may take me that long to recuperate from this one."

"Jordan and I did the food. You just had to organize the races."

"And line up all the animals. The sheep alone weren't easy to find." Zachary pressed his lips together.

Becca opened her mouth to say something, looked hard at her brother and frowned instead.

"Also think of all the extra lessons I had to give. I had

to make sure people knew what they were doing. Riding a sheep isn't like riding a horse." A gleam sparkled in his eyes as he winked at Jordan.

Becca playfully punched her brother in the arm. "I knew it. You've had a great time. So can I tell Nancy it's a yes for next April or May?"

"I won't hear the end of it if I say no, especially from my son. So yes."

"Great. That's all I needed to know." Becca hopped up and headed off toward a group of people by the barn.

"Are you one of those brothers who relished making his sister's life miserable when you two were growing up?"

"Isn't that what a little brother is for?"

"I wouldn't know. All I had is a big sis like you."

Nicholas ran across the yard toward them.

"I'd like Nicholas to stay over again tonight. We decided to lie out in the pasture where there are no city lights and study the stars. See how many we can count."

Spend the night again? If she wasn't homeschooling her son, she would never see him anymore.

Nicholas skidded to a stop at the end of the picnic table. "We're going to be in the field." He waved his hand toward an empty pasture to the left. "Some of the guys are putting together a touch football game, and I'm going to play."

Football? Until her son had gotten to know his father, he hadn't wanted anything to do with the sport, and she'd been thrilled by that. "Hon, you've never played before. I think you should sit this one out."

"But I want to play. I'm going to be on Randy's team. If I don't play, the sides won't be equal."

Jordan glanced from Nicholas to some of the larger boys gathering near the field her son indicated. He and Becca's oldest son were the smallest two on the teams. "I don't think so."

"Dad?" Nicholas glued his attention on Zachary. "Touch football isn't like regular football. I'll be okay. Tell Mom that."

Zachary looked toward Jordan. "There's no tackling in touch football. It's mostly running and trying to evade the opposing player. Nicholas would be good at that. He's pretty quick."

"Yeah, Mom, remember how well I did when we played soccer?"

"They aren't the same."

"Please." Nicholas wore his puppy-dog look.

Rising, she glared at Zachary. "Can we have a word?" She walked a few steps away from the picnic table and turned her back on Nicholas. When Zachary joined her, she lowered her voice. "He isn't equipped to play something like football, even touch football."

"Quit smothering *our* son. Other kids play and are perfectly fine. I used to play and there were no broken bones."

"I don't like this."

"What? The football or me having a say in what our son does?"

Both! She'd been the only caregiver for ten years and now all of sudden she was supposed to consult and share the decisions with Zachary. Acid burned her stomach. She skirted Zachary and marched back to the table. "If your dad thinks it's safe, then I'll—"

Nicholas threw his arms around her neck. "Thanks." Then he raced toward the field where the others were.

When Zachary approached, she muttered, "I've been manipulated," then strode toward a group cleaning up the eating area.

* * *

As Jordan stormed away, disconcerted, Zachary took his cowboy hat and dusted it off against his jeans, his hand clutching the Stetson. Everything had gone well today. Nicholas hadn't had a problem in any of his competitions, and yet Jordan insisted on being overprotective. She needed to back off, and he was going to make sure she realized that. He owed it to his son.

Then he thought of why Jordan was so protective of Nicholas. She'd had to face almost losing him—alone. He'd wished he'd been there to help her through the ordeal. Hold her. Comfort her.

The commotion of the teams preparing to play in the field drew his attention. Even though he understood where she was coming from, she still had to realize he was Nicholas's dad and had an equal say now in how their son was raised.

The participants of the touch football game formed their teams and lined up. Zachary stood against the fence, not far from the sideline they had marked with long links of rope. Two barrels at the ends of the pasture were the goal posts. Some of the parents, including Jordan, came to watch the impromptu scrimmage. She stood next to Becca several yards away from him and stared straight ahead. Her features formed a neutral expression, but even from this distance he felt her frustration and anger conveyed by the crossed arms and legs.

For the first fifteen minutes Nicholas hung back, not going after the person with the ball. Then suddenly one of the opposing players caught the ball near his son. He dashed after the thirteen-year-old and touched his arm. Nicholas jumped up and down. Randy came over and gave him a high five. His son's grin encompassed his whole face.

From that point on Nicholas became more involved. Several times he went after the ball carrier and once more tagged him. He was becoming more confident the more he did. First with riding, then roping. And now playing team sports like soccer and football. Zachary felt as if he'd accomplished something with his son—showed him how to play.

During the half his son ran over to him and took the bottle of water he handed him. "I'm not so bad."

"No, you're quick on your feet. You're doing good."

Nicholas made himself as tall as he could and raised his chin. "Mom worries too much."

"That's a mother's job." Although he had to agree with his son.

Nicholas glanced behind him. "Gotta go. We're starting the second half."

Zachary chuckled to himself. A month ago his son knew nothing about football until he watched some videos and read about it prior to the homecoming game.

The time flew by. The dad refereeing the game indicated a minute left. Nicholas's team had the ball and the quarterback stepped back to throw it. His intended receiver was delayed and Nicholas jumped up and caught the ball. When he came down with it clasped to him, he wobbled and paused to steady himself. An opposing team member running full force toward him noticed the delay and tried to stop. Instead he bowled right over Nicholas, flattened him on the ground. The ball shot up in the air. Someone snatched it and ran for a touchdown.

Nicholas remained down, not moving. Zachary's heartbeat accelerated as he jogged toward his son, Jordan a couple of feet in front of him. She knelt next to their son, Nicholas's chest rising and falling rapidly.

"Don't move." Her hands ran over his body. "Where does it hurt?"

"I'm fine," Nicholas said in a breathless voice, dragging air into his lungs.

"You don't sound fine."

Their son pushed his upper body to a sitting position. "Just winded. Did we get a touchdown?" Nicholas looked beyond Jordan to Zachary.

He stepped forward and knelt next to her. "Yes."

Nicholas grinned. "We won, Mom!"

"It's time for us to go home." Jordan put her arm around Nicholas's shoulders and helped him up.

"But I want to spend the night with Dad."

"Not tonight."

"Partner, why don't you go say goodbye to everyone."

"But, Dad—"

Zachary tossed his head toward the barn. "Your mom and I have something to discuss."

Nicholas heaved a sigh then trudged off the field toward his teammates near the fence celebrating their victory.

When their son was out of earshot, Zachary rounded on Jordan. "Why isn't he staying tonight? He's fine. Nothing happened to him."

"We don't know that for sure. He could have a mild concussion. I'm gonna keep an eye on him. If anything is wrong, I'm near the hospital. This isn't up for discussion." She pinched her lips together and narrowed her eyes.

"Yes, it is. He's my son, too."

"I've been his primary caregiver and that isn't gonna change."

He squeezed his hands shut then flexed them. He moved into her personal space, his face close to hers. "That's because you kept him a secret." He schooled his voice to an even level while inside anger boiled. He had so much time to make up, and she was standing in the way.

"There's nothing I can do to change the past and I'm tired of trying."

When she started to skirt him, he impeded her progress. "Do I have to speak to a lawyer about my rights as Nicholas's dad?"

The threat, unplanned, tumbled from his mouth, and the second she heard it, color drained from her face. Her pupils grew huge. One part of him wanted to take the words back. Another meant everything he said. Nicholas would be his only child and he intended to participate fully in his life.

Jordan froze for a few seconds then she backed away, her mouth hanging open, her eyes round. Whirling around, she fled across the field, grabbed their son and made her way toward her Camaro.

What have I done? He buried his face in his hands and kneaded his fingertips into his forehead.

Becca closed the distance between them. "What's going on? Jordan and Nicholas are leaving." She nodded toward them getting into the car. "What did you say to her?"

"I asked if I should contact a lawyer concerning my rights as Nicholas's father."

His sister drew in a sharp breath. "You didn't? Why did you say that? You two can work things out without bringing lawyers into it. How do you think Nicholas will feel?"

"This never should have been an issue. I should have known from the beginning. I could have married her. Nicholas would have had both a mother and father."

"Then do it now."

He stared at Jordan and Nicholas, his son's face set in a pout, her expression anger filled. "It's too late for us."

"Because you can't forgive her."

"I'm trying," he said, instead of explaining his turmoil over not being able to give her another child.

"Not hard enough."

Jordan backed up her car, then headed down the gravel road.

"Go after her. Don't leave it like that."

A lawyer! Zachary wants to get custody of Nicholas. All hope of them ever working something out vanished when she heard those words. There was nothing she could do to earn his forgiveness, to make him understand all she wanted was for him and Nicholas to be her family. She didn't care if he couldn't have any more children.

"Mom, why are we leaving? I want to stay." Nicholas clicked on his seat belt.

Fury jammed Jordan's throat and something she wished she didn't feel—the pain of loss. She drove toward the entrance to the ranch, tears stinging her eyes. "It was time to go. You hit the ground pretty hard. If you get a headache, become nauseated or dizzy, let me know immediately."

"I don't have a concussion. I'm fine."

Lord, I just want my old life back. At least I knew what to expect. I don't want to lose my son. I know I've made mistakes, but why couldn't Zachary, Nicholas and I be a family?

She pulled onto the highway. "Hon, you've been gone a lot lately. Nana and Granny have missed you. I missed you."

Nicholas remained quiet. Jordan slanted a look at him. A pout thinned his lips, his arms folded over his chest.

She'd get home and talk to Rachel. She just needed to get things back under her control.

Out of the corner of her eye, she saw something large and brown, moving fast, crossing the road only yards in front of her. A deer?

Zachary jumped in his truck and started out after Jordan. He shouldn't have said what he had about the lawyer. He might be angry with her, but that was hitting below the belt, and she didn't deserve it. She'd been a good mother to Nicholas.

He pressed down on the accelerator to catch up with her. Up ahead he spied her Camaro.

Then he saw the deer leap onto the highway right in front of Jordan's car. She swerved to avoid the animal and plowed off the road. Her vehicle bounced across the rough terrain and plunged into a ditch near the field, a tree stopping her forward motion. The medium-size oak swayed under the impact. His heartbeat stalled for a few seconds as his gaze fastened onto her car, the front end smashed against the trunk.

With his pulse thundering in his ears, he sped until he reached the place where Jordan went off the road. He slammed on his breaks and jumped from his truck. He raced toward the wreck. His pulse racing even faster than he was.

Lord, let them be alive. It can't end this way.

Reaching the rear bumper, he climbed into the ditch on the driver's side, nearest him. A gray cloud bellowed from the scrunched hood. He peered inside. Her head lay against the deflated airbag and steering wheel. He jerked on the door. He couldn't budge it.

Back up the ditch, he made his way to the other side and tried to get in. A fine powder floated inside the car. Nicholas, held up by his seat belt, sagged against the window, a spiderweb of cracks spreading out from the contact with his head. Blood ran down his face.

Panting, trying desperately to suppress the panic churning in his gut, Zachary yanked with all his strength on the handle. For a few seconds nothing happened. Then the door creaked open half a foot. He wedged his arm through the crack and pried it open farther.

"Nicholas. Jordan." His voice shook as much as his body did.

Jordan moaned and looked toward him. Blinking, she raised her head and reached toward their son. "No. Nicholas."

He stirred, his eyelids lifting partway. "Mom?" He tried to move and collapsed back.

"Stay still, son. I'm calling 911." Zachary dug for his cell and clenched it to keep the trembling in his hands from showing. After he reported the accident, he turned back to Jordan and his son. "Help is on the way."

"My leg hurts." Tears filled Nicholas's eyes and spilled over onto his cheeks, mingling with the blood.

Zachary inspected his son and noticed his left leg was pinned by the dashboard. Kneeling next to Nicholas, he took his hand. "You'll be all right. Just don't move."

Jordan tried her door. When she couldn't budge it, she twisted back toward Zachary. "I'm stuck."

The fright on her pale face, in her voice, tore at his composure. She tried to unhook her seat belt but couldn't. She shoved again at the door but it remained shut. When she looked at him, her panic drove the terror away.

"Easy, Jordan. The paramedics will be here soon." He stood and stared down the stretch of highway then stooped again. "I hear a siren. Five minutes tops." *Hurry. I can't lose them.*

"I need to help my son. I couldn't stop. I couldn't

avoid…" Her words faded into the quiet. She placed her hand on Nicholas's arm closest to her as though she could will her strength into him.

His own helplessness inundated Zachary. He rose again and watched for the ambulance. Flashing lights and the sound of the siren grew closer. The pounding of his heart nearly drowned out the approaching emergency vehicles. He'd never been so afraid in his life—even when the bull had crushed him.

"Everything is going to be okay," he murmured as much to reassure himself as Nicholas and Jordan.

Hours later, Jordan sat in the waiting room surrounded by family, Granny on one side and Rachel on the other. Her mother was nearby talking with Zachary and Becca, their voices too low to hear what they were saying.

Nicholas had just been taken into surgery to repair his broken leg. The scent of antiseptic knotted her stomach so tight bile clogged her throat. The sterile room, painted a light green, reminded her of the one in South Carolina. She'd almost lost her son then. This time he would be all right, but the feeling of being out of control bombarded her from all sides.

She leaped to her feet. She couldn't sit here any longer.

"Where are you going, honey?" her mother asked.

Glancing over her shoulder, Jordan locked gazes with Zachary for a few seconds before looking at her mom. "Out of here."

Zachary rose, concern in his expression. "I'll come with you."

"No!" She fled the room, tears shadowing her vision as she hurried down the hall toward she wasn't sure where.

The last thing she needed was Zachary to be kind to

her, to say anything to her. Since the paramedics and high-way patrol arrived on the scene of the wreck, everything happened in a blur as if she were watching it from afar. Separate. A spectator.

She wanted her old life back before she'd come to Tall-grass. Since her arrival home, nothing had been the same. Every day there was something new to deal with. She didn't know what to expect anymore—except that Zach-ary didn't really want to have anything to do with her. Only Nicholas.

The sign for the chapel drew her toward it. She entered and escaped inside the dimly lit room, nondescript, with several rows of chairs. The sounds of the hospital faded as she shut the door.

She collapsed onto the seat nearest to her and bowed her head. For the longest moment she couldn't think of anything to say to the Lord. Her son was hurting again because of something she'd done this time. She should have been able to avoid the accident. She should have been able...

The tears streaked down her face, released finally like a valve turned completely on unchecked. She let them fall into her lap. She'd walked away with a few cuts and bruises. Why couldn't she have been the one hurt, needing surgery? Not her son.

Why, Lord? What are You trying to tell me?

The door opened. Lifting her head, Jordan grew so stiff her muscles locked painfully. She needed to be alone. She needed— Granny slipped inside and came to sit beside her. Her grandmother patted Jordan's hands clutched together in her lap.

For minutes silence reigned in the chapel. The ham-mering of Jordan's heartbeat pulsated in her ears. Slowly her grandmother's presence blanketed Jordan in a calming mantle. God had sent Granny to comfort her.

"I've really made a mess of my life," she finally said, the heat from her grandmother's touch warming Jordan's cold body.

"Why do you say that? The wreck was an accident. From what Zachary said there wasn't anything you could have done. It happened so fast."

The mention of Zachary renewed her fear that he'd take her to court concerning custody of their son. The calming mantle slipped from her. "He wants Nicholas."

"Of course he does. He's his father. It's a good thing he wants to be in Nicholas's life."

"He told me he's gonna talk to a lawyer."

"When, child?"

"Today at the ranch right before I left."

"Do you trust in the Lord?"

"Yes." Jordan shifted toward her grandmother and saw the doubt in her eyes. "You don't think I do?"

"I believe you think you do, but you're always so busy trying to control everything in your life that you've lost sight of what's important. God knows what is best for us, and sometimes we have to just put our faith in Him. Trust Him, child, completely. He brought you back here for a reason. Quit fighting Him every step of the way."

"Control? Today I discovered I have no control really. Literally in a blink of an eye your life can change."

"My point exactly." Granny tapped her chest. "Take it from this eighty-one-years-young woman who has been through a lot in that time. Just when you think you've got everything figured out, something changes. Faith is what has sustained me. It can for you, too." Pushing to her feet, she gripped the back of the chair in front of her. "I imagine you've got some thinking and praying to do. I'll be in the waiting room."

Jordan stood and hugged her grandmother. "I love you. I'll be back in a little bit."

After Granny left, Jordan sank back down and clasped her hands. "Father, I've been so wrong. I've been scared to trust anyone—You, Zachary. There's always been a part I've held back. Please help me. I need You."

"Nicholas is gonna be all right, Zachary." Becca paused next to him at the vending machine.

He punched the button for coffee. Its scent wafted to him as the cup filled. He'd always loved the smell of coffee. Now it seared a hole in his gut. "I'll feel better when the doctor tells me. Remember what happened to me when the bull trampled me?"

"This is different. Not nearly as complicated." His sister checked her watch. "In fact, the surgery should be over soon."

"I can't help wondering if what I said to Jordan right before she left didn't contribute to the wreck."

"You told me you saw it and it happened so fast there wasn't anything she could have done except swerve or hit the buck. Hitting the deer would have caused major damage, too. Remember that time Dad ran into a cow? The insurance company totaled our car."

"I know." He dragged his fingers through his hair, kneading his fingers into his taut neck muscles. "But I really didn't mean I would contact a lawyer. I was angry and lashed out at Jordan. She left upset...." He couldn't shake the image of her car going off the road or the picture of Jordan and Nicholas hurt and trapped. Helplessness flooded him again as if a downpour deluged him.

"Then talk with her and tell her you didn't mean it. Ask her forgiveness."

He flinched. "How can I ask her to do that when I've had trouble doing that myself?"

"What would have happened if Jordan had really hurt herself or worse—died? How would you have felt holding on to that anger over something that happened years ago? Does your anger make you feel better? Or is it Audrey you're really mad at? Forgive both of them."

His sister's words made him think about the unthinkable. Had his relationship with Audrey colored his with Jordan? What if Jordan had died today? The very thought chilled his blood. A world without her? He shuddered, one wave after another rippling down his body.

"You've got more than yourself to consider now. What are you teaching your son if you hold a grudge like you are? If she can forgive Mom, why can't you forgive her?"

Zachary took the coffee cup and sipped at the hot brew. A bitter taste coated his tongue that had nothing to do with his drink and everything to do with the picture of the kind of man he was showing his son.

Rachel came around the corner. "Zachary, Nicholas is out of surgery. The doctor is in the waiting room."

A few hours later Jordan stood outside Nicholas's hospital room. "Mom, I'm staying here tonight."

"Honey, I'm worried about you. You look exhausted."

"I couldn't sleep even if I was at home. If all goes well, Nicholas will come home soon. Then I can get some rest."

Her mother squeezed her hand. "I understand. I'll see you all in the morning."

Jordan watched her mom and grandmother get on the elevator before she turned back toward her son's door.

Everyone was gone except Zachary. She'd been able to manage being in the same room with him as long as others were there, too.

She entered, her gaze immediately seeking the bed where Nicholas slept. He'd wakened briefly after the surgery but was now sleeping soundly. His bandaged head underscored what had happened earlier.

Again the picture of the buck flashed into her mind. It had been too close for her to do anything but swerve or hit it. Neither option had been good. The sounds of the crash—the crunch of her car folding like an accordion, the airbag exploding outward—and the smells of the leaking engine fluids mingling with the stagnant water in the ditch assailed her. Goose bumps rose on her arms, and she hugged them to her.

Zachary cleared his throat, reminding her she wasn't alone. Wouldn't be the whole night because he was staying with his son, too. Exhausted, aching, she didn't know if she could deal with another incident where they dueled over Nicholas. Why couldn't he leave and come back with the rest in the morning? She'd always been the one in the past to stay, holding vigilance. But wasn't that the problem?

Zachary should have had that choice all those years ago. She turned away, not wanting him to see the conflict that had to be written on her face. He couldn't forgive her, so as most things, this was out of her control. *Lord, Your will*.

With Zachary on the small couch, she moved to the chair a few feet away. She turned it to point toward Nicholas's bed. Taking a seat, her back to Zachary, she closed her eyes and inhaled deep breaths to calm her stressed body. But nothing relieved the tension that bunched every muscle.

The hairs on her nape tingled right before Zachary's hand covered her clenched one on the armrest. "I'll sit here if you want to lie down on the couch."

His warm touch shot up her arm, burning through any defenses she scrambled to erect. She couldn't take another rejection. Not today. "I'm fine," she managed to say through parched lips, her throat so dry the words squeaked out.

He moved in front of her and squatted. "No, you aren't. You were in a wreck, too. I imagine your body is starting to feel the effects of it."

"Don't do this. Don't make…" Her throat closed completely around any other words she tried to say.

"I think we need to talk."

"No, not now. I have enough to handle without you letting me know I put our child in danger. He's there because of me. I—"

Zachary drew her up and pulled her into his embrace. "You aren't at fault. Don't do that to yourself."

She resisted the lure of his arms, jerking back. "If I hadn't left when I did or gone a little faster or slower, Nicholas wouldn't have been hurt."

"What-ifs don't change the situation and only make you upset. Freak accidents happen to people."

Her jammed tears swelled into her eyes. She blinked, releasing them. "I know. I can't control everything like I've wanted. That point has been hammered home to me today painfully. But why couldn't I have been the one in that bed? Not my son."

"*Our* son." He brushed his thumbs over her cheeks, erasing the tears only to have them replaced immediately. Framing her face, he inched closer. "We are in this together."

Not really and that was the problem. She wanted all of Zachary. She wanted the complete family. He didn't. She'd messed it all up. Straightening, she attempted a smile that fell flat. "I appreciate your concern. I'll be okay, especially when I can get Nicholas home."

He tugged her toward the couch, gently pushed her down

then sat beside her. "We still need to talk. Earlier today I didn't mean what I said about getting a lawyer."

Tension, even more than before, whipped down her length. "Maybe for the time being, but will you use that threat later when we clash about Nicholas?"

"I know we can work something out. You want what's best for Nicholas, and so do I."

He hadn't answered her question, which clinched her stomach into a snarl of emotions. She curled her hands at her sides. She loved him. And couldn't have him.

He slid his arm along the back of the couch, loosely cocooning her against him. "I'm not doing a very good job of explaining myself."

"Oh, I think I know where you stand."

He leaned closer, putting his thumb under her chin and turning her head so she looked straight at him. "Do you? Because until recently I didn't realize what I was doing. How harmful my attitude was."

"What do you mean?"

"I let my anger purposely make you mad. You fled. If I hadn't said that to you, we might have been able to work everything out earlier today, and Nicholas wouldn't be lying there."

"Didn't you just tell me we can't play what-ifs?"

"Yes, but see how I can twist it around to be my fault? It really was no one's." He stared at his son for a long moment. "When you came back to Tallgrass and told me I was a father, I was furious at you. At first, all I could see was the ten years you'd stolen from me."

She opened her mouth to apologize again, but he placed his finger over her lips.

A lopsided tilt to his mouth filled her vision. "I know you're sorry for what happened, but I was being stubborn and not listening to what you really said. I was letting what happened with my fiancée affect us. You aren't Audrey. When I turn the situation around and look at it differently, I'm so grateful to you for giving me a son even if it was ten years late. You didn't have to tell me. Then I would never know the joy of being a father. You've given me that joy and for that I thank you."

"You forgive me?"

"More than that. I love you, Jordan. I've never really stopped. We were both young and said and did things we regret. I can't keep living in the past. I want a future with you and Nicholas. I want a family. I could have lost you today. That can change a person's perspective real fast." He cupped her face. "Can you forgive me? Will you accept me in your life even though Nicholas will be the only child we have?"

His questions hovered suspended in the air between them for several heartbeats. For a second she wondered if she'd heard him correctly or was it her weary mind playing tricks on her.

"I know you have a right to be mad at me. I—"

Jordan placed her fingers over his mouth. "Shh." Winding her arms around him, she drew him toward her and kissed him with all her heart.

"I want to do what we should have done years ago. Will you marry me as soon as possible? Make me happy? Make our son happy?"

She combed her fingers through his hair and slanted his head toward hers again. "Yes." She planted a peck on one corner of his mouth. "Yes." Another kiss on the other side. "And yes. You and Nicholas are my life." Her lips covered his with the promise of more to come.

Epilogue

"It's taken us a long time to get here, but we've finally gotten it right, Mrs. Rutgers." Zachary locked his arms around Jordan.

"Say that again." She cuddled closer.

"Mrs. Rutgers."

"I don't think I'll ever get tired of hearing that name."

He smiled. "That's great since you'll have it for say fifty or so years." Leaning forward, he kissed her thoroughly.

Someone coughed behind Jordan. She blushed and turned within her husband's embrace.

"Save that for the honeymoon." Granny winked. "Right now you two have guests to see to."

Jordan scanned the reception hall at the church. All their friends were crammed into the large room. The new ones she'd met through Helping Hands Homeschooling group and the old ones she'd grown up with. But besides Nicholas and her family, the two she was happiest to see attending her and Zachary's wedding was his parents.

"Oh, I see Doug is getting seconds. I'd better corral him before his cholesterol shoots up." Granny shuffled off to the right.

"How long do you think it will be before Doug and Granny marry?" Zachary whispered against her ear.

"I hope soon. Her and Mom are fighting again."

"Speaking of mothers, are you really okay with Mom taking Nicholas to Arizona for the week while we're on our honeymoon?"

Jordan caught sight of her son, in a leg cast but mobile, talking with Zachary's parents. "Totally. Your mother and I had a long talk last night. All we both want is what is best for you and Nicholas. We're on the same page."

A twinkle sparkled in his eyes. "Good. Can we sneak away now? I want to start the honeymoon."

"Sounds like a perfect game plan."

* * * * *

Dear Reader,

I had so much fun creating the story of Jordan and Zachary, high school sweethearts who parted and were forced to be together again because of their child. This is a book about forgiveness and trust, which are so important in a relationship. Both Jordan and Zachary had to deal with both of these issues.

Also in *Heart of a Cowboy,* Nicholas didn't flourish in school although he was very smart. He stifled his intelligence because the other children made fun of him. This is a reason some parents homeschool their children. In each book in the series I want to try to show a different situation that leads to parents deciding to homeschool.

I love hearing from readers. You can contact me at margaretdaley@gmail.com or at P.O. Box 2074 Tulsa, OK 74101. You can also learn more about my books at www.margaretdaley.com. I have a quarterly newsletter that you can sign up for on my Web site or you can enter my monthly drawings by signing my guest book.

Best wishes,

Margaret Daley

QUESTIONS FOR DISCUSSION

1. Zachary couldn't forgive Jordan for not telling him about his son. His past ruled his life. Do you have something that has happened in your past that has done that to you? How can you get past that?

2. Who was your favorite character ? Why?

3. Why is it important to forgive others and ourselves? What happens when we live in the past rather than look forward to the future? Which do you focus on—past, present or future? Why?

4. Jordan was afraid of losing her son to the point she was overprotective. Have you ever done that? How did you handle it?

5. What was your favorite scene? Why?

6. Jordan knew she'd made a mistake concerning Zachary and Nicholas and regretted it. Have you ever made the kind of mistake you felt that you paid for more than most? How did you deal with it?

7. Jordan thought if she could control her life then she would be all right. She didn't realize there are a lot of things we can't control in our lives. What are some things that have happened to you lately that have been out of your control? How did you deal with them?

8. Nicholas was very smart and learned quickly, but he

hated to write and avoided it as much as possible. Have you ever avoided something you couldn't do well? What happened when you had to do it?

9. Zachary loved taking risks like bull riding in a rodeo. Do you take risks? Why or why not?

10. Although Zachary knew he should forgive Jordan, that God wanted him to, he couldn't. Have you ever done something you knew you shouldn't? How did the situation turn out by avoiding what you knew you should do?

11. Granny was Jordan's mentor. Jordan turned to Granny for advice. Do you have a mentor? Who is it and why is that person your mentor?

12. Jordan kept a secret for more than ten years. Secrets often have a way of coming out. When she came back home, she had to face the secret she'd kept. When it came out, she had to face the consequences. Has that happened to you? What did you do?

13. Jordan's mom was treating Granny as if she were a child rather than her mother. How do you treat your parents? Do health issues affect your interaction with your parents?

14. Nicholas wrote an essay about the disappearing cowboy—an ideal from our past. Do you agree with him? Why or why not?

15. Both Jordan and Zachary wondered what would have happened if Zachary's mother had passed on the

messages from Jordan. Do you ever wonder if something would have happened differently in your past, where you would be today? Is it good to wonder what-ifs in our lives? Why or why not?

TITLES AVAILABLE NEXT MONTH

Available July 27, 2010

LARGER-PRINT BOOKS!

GET 2 FREE LARGER-PRINT NOVELS PLUS 2 FREE MYSTERY GIFTS

Larger-print novels are now available...

YES! Please send me 2 FREE LARGER-PRINT Love Inspired® novels and my 2 FREE mystery gifts (gifts are worth about $10). After receiving them, if I don't wish to receive any more books, I can return the shipping statement marked "cancel." If I don't cancel, I will receive 6 brand-new novels every month and be billed just $4.74 per book in the U.S. or $5.24 per book in Canada. That's a saving of over 20% off the cover price. It's quite a bargain! Shipping and handling is just 50¢ per book.* I understand that accepting the 2 free books and gifts places me under no obligation to buy anything. I can always return a shipment and cancel at any time. Even if I never buy another book, the two free books and gifts are mine to keep forever. .

122/322 IDN E7QP

Name	(PLEASE PRINT)
Address	Apt. #
City	State/Prov.	Zip/Postal Code

Signature (if under 18, a parent or guardian must sign)

Mail to Steeple Hill Reader Service:
IN U.S.A.: P.O. Box 1867, Buffalo, NY 14240-1867
IN CANADA: P.O. Box 609, Fort Erie, Ontario L2A 5X3

Not valid to current subscribers to Love Inspired Larger-Print books.

**Are you a current subscriber to Love Inspired books and want to receive the larger-print edition?
Call 1-800-873-8635 or visit www.morefreebooks.com.**

* Terms and prices subject to change without notice. Prices do not include applicable taxes. Sales tax applicable in N.Y. Canadian residents will be charged applicable provincial taxes and GST. Offer not valid in Quebec. This offer is limited to one order per household. All orders subject to approval. Credit or debit balances in a customer's account(s) may be offset by any other outstanding balance owed by or to the customer. Please allow 4 to 6 weeks for delivery. Offer available while quantities last.

Your Privacy: Steeple Hill Books is committed to protecting your privacy. Our Privacy Policy is available online at www.SteepleHill.com or upon request from the Reader Service. From time to time we make our lists of customers available to reputable third parties who may have a product or service of interest to you. If you would prefer we not share your name and address, please check here. ☐

Help us get it right—We strive for accurate, respectful and relevant communications. To clarify or modify your communication preferences, visit us at www.ReaderService.com/consumerschoice.

LILP10R

Five hunky Texas single fathers—five stories from Cathy Gillen Thacker's LONE STAR DADS *miniseries. Here's an excerpt from the latest,* THE MOMMY PROPOSAL *from Harlequin American Romance.*

"I hear you work miracles," Nate Hutchinson drawled. Brooke Mitchell had just stepped into his lavishly appointed office in downtown Fort Worth, Texas.

"Sometimes, I do." Brooke smiled and took the sexy financier's hand in hers, shook it briefly.

"Good." Nate looked her straight in the eye. "Because I'm in need of a home makeover—fast. The son of an old friend is coming to live with me."

She was still tingling from the feel of his warm palm. "Temporarily or permanently?"

"If all goes according to plan, I'll adopt Landry by summer's end."

Brooke had heard the founder of Nate Hutchinson Financial Services was eligible, wealthy and generous to a fault. She hadn't known he was in the market for a family, but she supposed she shouldn't be surprised. But Brooke had figured a man as successful and handsome as Nate would want one the old-fashioned way. *Not that this was any of her business...*

"So what's the child like?" she asked crisply, trying not to think how the marine-blue of Nate's dress shirt deepened the hue of his eyes.

"I don't know." Nate took a seat behind his massive antique mahogany desk. He relaxed against the smooth leather of the chair. "I've never met him."

"Yet you've invited this kid to live with you permanently?"

"It's complicated. But I'm sure it's going to be fine."

Obviously Nate Hutchinson knew as little about teenage